Vlad the Drac Vampire

This is the fourth book in the stories of the miniature vegetarian vampire, Vlad the Drac.

When Vlad hears that Judy and Paul have a new baby sister, he loses no time at all in rushing over to London to help and to be the baby's vampire god-father. As usual Vlad's arrival plunges the Stone family into total chaos.

To keep Vlad out of mischief around the house, Mum suggests that the children take him sight-seeing round London. But all the trouble Vlad causes at home is nothing to what he can manage on the town!

An entertaining and funny book.

Other Books by Ann Jungman

Vlad the Drac · *Barn Owl Books*

Vlad the Drac Returns · *Barn Owl Books*

Vlad the Drac Superstar · *Barn Owl Books*

Lucy and the Big Bad Wolf · *Barn Owl Books*

Bold Bad Ben The Beastly Bandit · *Barn Owl Books*

Leila's Magical Monster Party · *Barn Owl Books*

Over the Rainbow · *Oxford University Press*

Resistance · *Barrington Stoke*

Siege · *Barrington Stoke*

Bacillus and the Beastly Bath · *A & C Black*

Clottus and the Ghostly Gladiator · *A & C Black*

Tertius and the Humble Hunt · *A & C Black*

Twitta and the Ferocious Fever · *A & C Black*

The Most Magnificent Mosque · *Frances Lincoln*

Broomstick Services · *Happy Cat Books*

Broomstick Removals · *Happy Cat Books*

Broomstick Rescues · *Happy Cat Books*

Broomstick Baby · *Happy Cat Books*

Septimouse Supermouse · *Happy Cat Books*

Saptimouse Big Cheese · *Happy Cat Books*

Septimouse and the Cheese Party · *Happy Cat Booke*

Ann Jungman

VLAD THE DRAC
VAMPIRE

ILLUSTRATED BY GEORGE THOMPSON

BARN OWL BOOKS

To Judy and Carole with love

Vlad the Drac Vampire was first published by Young Lions in 1988
This edition was published in 2006 by Barn Owl Books
157 Fortis Green Road, London N10 3LX
Barn Owl Books are distributed by Frances Lincoln
4 Torriano Mews, Torriano Avenue, London NW5 2RZ
Text copyright © 1988, 2006 Ann Jungman
Illustrations copyright © 1988, 2006 George Thompson

ISBN 1-903015-55-3

Designed and typeset by Douglas Martin
Printed in China for Imago

Contents

Contents

I

The Godfather

Judy and Paul sat by the phone looking at each other.

'What do you want it to be?' asked Paul. 'A boy or a girl?'

'I don't think I mind,' replied Judy. 'But whichever it is, 'I wish it would hurry up and come.'

At that moment the phone rang. Paul grabbed it.

'Hi Dad, yes, a girl, great, wonderful!'

Judy pulled the phone from him. 'How's Mum? Good. Great, super, brill. Give her our love and we'll come and see the baby tomorrow.'

'Well,' said Paul as she hung up. 'We've got a sister.'

'Umm,' said Judy. 'Isn't it exciting! I wish I could tell someone.'

'Yes,' agreed Paul. 'It would be nice to share the news, but Dad will phone Gran and all the relatives.'

'I know,' suggested Judy, 'let's tell Vlad.'

'We could, I suppose,' said Paul. 'But Romania is a long way.'

'But he *is* like one of the family,' insisted Judy. 'Even Dad agreed to that when you were in hospital.'

'That's true,' said Paul. 'All right, let's phone him. After all, the birth of a new Stone is pretty important news.'

So they found Vlad's phone number and looked in the telephone directory for information on how to make an international call.

'Here it is,' said Paul. 'Look, for Romania you dial 00 40 and then the person's number.'

'The vampire's number,' corrected Judy.

So they rang through and waited for Vlad to answer. At last they heard someone pick up the phone.

'Could I speak to Vlad the Drac, please' said Paul.

'I hope they speak English,' whispered Judy.

A few moments later there was a click.

'Count Dracula's castle, Vlad the Drac speaking.'

'Vlad, it's Paul here. Mum's had a baby, a little girl. We've got a new sister.'

'A baby!' shrieked Vlad. 'A real live human baby? That's wonderful. Why did no one tell me what was happening? I'd have come over to help.'

'That's very nice of you, Vlad, but there's nothing to do.'

'Nothing to do! You wait till you've had five

children, there'll be less of the nothing to do. Now you tell everyone to hold their horses, help is coming.'

'But Vlad, we only wanted to tell you about the baby. We don't need any help.'

'You're being very selfish as usual, Paul. Of course *you* don't need any help, but I'm sure Mum could do with an extra pair of hands. Anyway, I want to be the baby's vampire godfather.'

'Vlad says he's going to come over to help,' whispered Paul to his sister. 'Think of something to say to stop him.'

'Hello Vlad,' said Judy, taking the phone. 'Yes, it is lovely news, isn't it?'

'Did Paul tell you that I'm catching the next plane to London?'

'Well, yes, Vlad, he did'.

'Well, aren't you thrilled? Aren't you delighted?'

'It's a lovely idea, Vlad, but I think Mum might want just the family here when she comes home.'

'And what, pray, do you call me? Am I not family? Really, Judy, you are very silly sometimes. Now, I expect it of Paul but not of you. I am very experienced with children, being the father of five, and I will be an invaluable help to your dear Mother, so tell her to expect me.'

'But Vlad, Gran's coming to stay and she's very experienced with children too.'

'Cancel her,' insisted Vlad, 'Vampire nannies are the best. Don't bother to come to the airport, I'll make my own way over to you.'

Judy looked at Paul in despair.

'He's hung up and he's coming.'

Paul groaned. 'Dad will never forgive us. Can you imagine a new baby *and* Vlad?'

'If we phoned him back and said that it was all a joke and that there isn't any new baby, do you think that would stop him?' suggested Judy desperately.

'No,' said Paul gloomily. 'It's too late, nothing will stop him now.'

'Let's toss for which one of us is going to tell Dad,' said Judy.

'All right,' agreed Paul, and took a coin out of his pocket. 'Heads or tails?'

Judy was just about to say tails, when the phone went again. Paul picked it up.

'It's Dad,' he whispered.

'You two have been on the phone for hours,' came Dad's voice. 'Who were you talking to?'

'No one,' said Paul vaguely.

'Huh,' replied his father. 'Well, look, I'm coming

home to fetch you two and take you out to supper and then we'll all pop in and see Mum and the baby before they both go to sleep. Be ready at the gate and you can just jump into the car.'

Judy and Paul quickly grabbed their coats and ran out of the house. While they were waiting for their father they discussed who was going to tell him about Vlad.

'Let's toss a penny tomorrow,' said Judy. 'I don't want to think about it tonight. I want to think about the baby.'

'Fair enough,' agreed Paul, as the car swept round the corner. Dad took the children to a Chinese restaurant where they had a long leisurely meal, and then up to the hospital.

'Can we see the baby?' asked Judy.

'Sure,' said Dad. 'But only for a minute. Mum's very tired. Just say 'Hello' and have a peep at your new sister.'

So Paul and Judy crept in and gave Mum a big hug. The baby was fast asleep.

'She's super,' said Paul.

'Yes,' agreed Judy. 'She's the best baby in the world.'

'Of course,' said Mum. 'Did you expect anything else? Now off you go and I'll see you tomorrow.'

As they drove home, Dad yawned.

'I'm exhausted,' he told the children. 'I haven't been so knackered for years. I'm really looking forward to a good night's sleep,' and he yawned again. Soon they were outside the house. Dad locked the car and Judy ran up to the front door to open it. She had got the key in the lock when a familiar voice said:

'Very nice of you to come back, I must say. Most considerate.'

Judy swung round and saw Vlad sitting on a small suitcase on the step.

'Vlad! I didn't see you.'

'So I noticed – you nearly crushed me. Poor Old Vlad, Poor Little Drac.'

'Judy,' groaned Paul. 'Tell me I didn't hear what I thought I heard.'

'You did,' said Judy. 'He's here, look.'

'Oh no,' moaned Paul.

'I've come all the way from Romania,' complained Vlad, 'and this is no sort of welcome. Poor Old Vlad, Poor Little Drac.'

Dad came up the front path.

'You know, I must really be tired, I'm hearing things. I thought I heard "Poor Old Vlad, Poor Little Drac".'

'You did,' said Paul nervously. 'He's here.'

'I most certainly am,' said Vlad. 'And I think you're all being very rude. I am happy to say that I have never met a vampire with such bad manners and I hope I never will. If Great Uncle Ghitza were here now he'd vampirise you all on the spot and good riddance.'

'Oh dear,' said Dad. 'Well, you'd better come in. We'll have to sort this out tomorrow because right now nothing, not even you, is going to keep me from my bed.' And he stomped off upstairs and slammed the door.

'Huh,' said Vlad sourly. 'Some people never change.'

'He's very tired,' said Judy. 'He was up all last night. I'm sure he's pleased to see you really.'

'And so he should be,' continued Vlad. 'I come all the way to London at great personal expense and inconvenience just 'cos Mum has had a baby and no one shows any appreciation.'

'It's just that we weren't expecting you, Vlad,' said Paul. 'It's such a surprise. Shall I bring your case in?'

'Thanks,' said Vlad, a little mollified.

'Would you like something to eat?' asked Judy. 'You must be tired after your long journey.'

'I am,' agreed Vlad. 'And cold from sitting on your doorstep.'

'Right,' said Judy. 'I'll heat up some washing-up liquid for you.'

'That,' said Vlad, 'would be very nice. At last someone has remembered their manners.'

'Good,' said Paul. 'So you won't need to say "Poor Old Vlad, Poor Little Drac" again.'

'No,' agreed Vlad. 'But I might say it anyway – just for fun.'

Soon they were sitting round the kitchen table. Paul and Judy drank hot chocolate and Vlad tucked into his hot washing-up liquid.

'This is just like the good old days,' commented Vlad. 'Just the three of us. Do you remember the first time I came to London and I was a big secret?'

'Yes,' said Judy. 'That was fun.'

'What I remember,' said Paul, 'is how scared we were that Vlad would get caught and put in the zoo or a museum.'

'Ah,' said Vlad. 'But I was destined for greater things. I became a film star and the father of five and the very most famous vampire in the whole world.'

'That's right,' agreed Judy. 'But you were very lucky not to end up in a zoo or a museum.'

'I prefer to look at it a bit differently,' said Vlad. 'I think they were unfortunate not to have me.'

'Maybe,' Said Judy yawning. 'I suppose we'd better go to bed.'

'Bed!' said Vlad in an outraged tone. 'Bed – but I've only just got here!'

'How *did* you do it so quickly?' demanded Paul. 'We didn't expect you till tomorrow – we didn't even have a chance to break the news to Dad.'

'So I noticed,' said Vlad sourly. 'Well, vampires travel very fast when need be. After all, it's only two hours by plane from Bucharest. Why you think it should take me two days, I cannot imagine. So when am I going to see my godchild?'

'We're going tomorrow,' Judy told him.

'Not tonight?' asked Vlad in a disappointed tone. 'Now that I've had a hot drink, I feel much better and I want to go now.'

'Well, you can't,' said Paul firmly. 'Mum's gone to sleep.'

'Poor Old Vlad, Poor Little Drac,' moaned the vampire. 'I want to see the snoglet.'

'The what?' asked Judy and Paul.

'The snoglet.' repeated Vlad. 'It's my name for the new baby.'

'Oh,' said Paul. 'I don't know if Mum will like that.'

'I like it,' said Judy. 'The snoglet, yes, it's a nice name for a baby.'

'You're a bright girl, Judy,' said the vampire. 'I've always said so. Now, whose drawer am I to sleep in tonight?'

'Mine!' yelled Judy.

'Mine!' shrieked Paul.

'Quietly, children, quietly,' said Vlad. 'We don't want to wake the Lord High up.' That was Vlad's name for Paul and Judy's father. 'Well, I suppose you'll have to toss a coin, to see which of you will have the honour of accommodating me tonight.'

'Heads or tails, Judy?' asked Paul, for the second time that day.

'Heads,' said Judy.

'Heads it is,' Paul told them.

'That's a very good way of settling a problem,' said Vlad proudly. 'I bet neither of you would have thought of tossing a coin.' And he flew on to Judy's shoulder to go upstairs. 'It just goes to show that you need a vampire around the place to sort out even the simplest of disputes.'

2

The Trunk

The next morning Judy and Vlad went downstairs for breakfast. Judy was halfway through her cornflakes and Vlad was battling with a tin of furniture polish, when Dad staggered down to join them.

'Shall I make some tea, Dad?' asked Paul as he joined them.

'No, coffee, black coffee, please. So it wasn't a nightmare I had last night; you really are here, Vlad.'

'Yes, I really am,' replied the vampire disdainfully. 'I came all the way from Romania when I heard the news about the snoglet.'

'The what?' asked Dad.

'The snoglet,' replied Vlad patiently. 'Your new daughter, my godchild.'

'Oh,' said Dad. 'You mean you've come all this way to be the snoglet – I mean my daughter's god-father?'

'That's right,' agreed Vlad, licking the very last hints

of polish out of the tin. 'Every child should have a vampire godfather – so much more useful these days than a fairy godmother.'

'Well, I don't know,' said Dad, taking a piece of toast. 'And why do you call the baby the snoglet?'

'"Cos I do,' said Vlad. 'I think it's a very nice name for a baby until it has a name of its own.'

'Well, I don't know about all this,' complained Dad.' And who told you about the – er – snoglet, anyway?'

'I was phoned,' announced Vlad. 'Two people, who shall be nameless, phoned me and said they had a brand new sister.'

'It was my idea, Dad,' confessed Judy. 'I wanted to tell someone.'

'I agreed,' interrupted Paul nobly. 'After all Vlad is one of the family, even you agreed to that.'

'It was in a minute of weakness,' declared Dad.

'You don't want me here,' wailed Vlad, beginning to cry. 'Poor Old Vlad, Poor Little Drac.'

'You promised not to say that,' yelled Dad. 'I've got it in writing on a piece of paper, signed by you.'

'That only applied to the last visit,' Vlad corrected him. 'This time I can say it as often as I like and I will if you don't agree to let me see the snoglet today.'

'Oh, all right,' groaned Dad. 'I'm not going to bother to have a fight with you.'

'Oh,' said Vlad, sounding a bit disappointed. 'Why not?'

'Because I notice that you only have a very small case, so I am assuming that you won't be staying very long.'

'Not at all,' Vlad assured him. 'My trunk is following, either today or tomorrow.'

'Oh no!' said Dad, burying his head in his hands.

'I've come to help out,' Vlad explained. 'As the father of five, I'm very experienced with babies.'

'I'm also very experienced with babies,' snapped Dad. 'It's kind of you to offer but we don't need you.'

'You've only had two so far,' replied Vlad. 'I have raised *five* little vampires and thus am more suited than you to looking after this snoglet.'

'I can't argue about it now,' said Dad, looking at his watch and grabbing his coat. 'We've got to get over to the hospital.'

So they all drove over to see Mum, who was very surprised to see Vlad. Vlad flew over to the cot where the baby was sleeping.

'Ooo, she's lovely,' he whispered. 'Look at her little hands and her little fingers and her little face.

Oh, she's super, a real little snoglet.'

'I thought you didn't like people,' commented Paul.

'I don't,' Vlad assured him. 'But I do like babies, human babies, vampire babies, all babies, and particularly I like this snoglet.'

'I'm glad you like our new baby,' smiled Mum. 'I rather like her myself.'

'That's very right and proper and as it should be,' commented Vlad. 'Mrs Vlad felt exactly the same about each of our five. Yes, I remember when Dad was born . . .'

'You do *not* remember when I was born,' interrupted Dad.

'Not *you*,' replied Vlad scornfully. 'My son Dad, the one I named after you before I discovered how horrible you were.'

'Now, now, you two,' said Mum.

'What are you going to call the baby?' asked Judy, quickly changing the subject.

'I rather like Hannah,' said Mum. 'What name would you like?'

'Madonna,' said Paul.

'Don't be silly,' said Dad.

'Well, what name would you suggest?' Paul demanded of his father.

'Sophie,' said Dad.

'Not bad,' agreed Judy. 'Or what about Zoë?'

'Hopeless,' said Vlad. 'Hopeless, you're all hopeless. She should be called by a good vampire name.'

'Like what?' demanded Dad.

'Like Vlad,' said the vampire casually.

'She's a girl!' yelled Dad.

'So she is,' agreed Vlad. 'Then let's call her Vladivostock.'

'That's not a name,' protested Mum. 'It's a town, a town in Russia.'

'Yes,' snapped Dad. 'And while we're about it why don't we call her Bournemouth or Southend-on-Sea or East Grinstead.'

'Ummm,' said Vlad, thinking hard. 'Yes, Southend-on-Sea isn't bad, it has a certain ring about it.'

'Don't be ridiculous,' yelled all the Stones.

'Sorry I spoke,' sniffed Vlad and went off into a corner to have a sulk.

'Poor Old Vlad, Poor Little Drac,' chorused the Stones.

'Quite wrong,' replied the vampire. 'Poor Old Drac, Poor Little Vlad.'

At that moment the baby let out a shriek.

'We still haven't given her a name,' said Judy. 'And she's protesting.'

'Poor little snoglet,' said Vlad, flying over the cot. 'We're neglecting you, aren't we?'

'Yes,' said Dad. 'And it's all your fault.'

Mum coughed. 'Nick, dear, we still haven't decided on a name.'

'How about Zoë Louise?' suggested Dad.

'It's all right,' said Paul.

'Very nice,' agreed Judy.

'I like it,' said Mum. 'And look at the baby, she's smiling. I think she likes it too. So that's settled.'

'Well,' commented Vlad. 'I don't see why you have to be mean about it. Why don't you call her Zoë Louise Snoglet Vladivostock Stone and when she is grown up, she can choose which one she wants.'

'If you think that I am going to tell the Registrar of Births that my daughter is called Zoë Louise Snoglet Vladivostock Stone you've got another think coming,' announced Dad.

'All right,' said Vlad, sighing deeply. 'Ignore my wishes, overrule me if you must, but one day I will tell her about the wonderful name she missed out on and I am sure she will be very cross. Judith, I am ready to go, you may take me home.' And with his nose in the air Vlad left the room on Judy's shoulder. Dad drove them home in silence; he put the children and Vlad down and drove straight back to the hospital. Outside the house was a strange car.

'It's Gran's car,' shrieked Judy. 'Oh good.'

'Great,' said Paul.

'And who is this Gran you're so pleased to see?' asked Vlad sourly. 'Is it the one I had to bite?'

'No,' explained Paul, as he opened the front door.' 'That was Mum's mum, this is Dad's mum.'

'Oh,' said Vlad. 'The Lord High's mater, what? I bet I don't get on with her.'

'Course you'll get on with Gran,' said Judy. 'Everyone loves her and you will too.'

'I wouldn't rely on it,' replied Vlad as they entered the house.

'Gran,' shrieked Judy and Paul, as they rushed to give their grandmother a hug.

'Hello you two,' said Gran smiling. 'Lovely to see you both and congratulations on your new sister.'

'She's lovely,' said Judy.

'I'm sure she is,' said Gran. 'As I've only just arrived, I haven't had time to meet her yet.'

24

'Well, I certainly hope you've got time to meet me,' came Vlad's voice.

'Who was that?' asked Gran in surprise.

'It is I,' declared Vlad, standing to his full height on Paul's shoulder. 'It is I, Vlad the Drac.'

'Oh dear,' said Gran, stepping back in shock.

'It's okay,' Judy assured her. 'He's quite safe, he's a tame vampire.'

'It's not that,' said Gran.

'Then *what* is it?' demanded Vlad.

'It's just that as I arrived, some men turned up with a trunk for a Mr V. Drac and I said that no one of that name lived here.'

'She's just like the Lord High,' yelled Vlad. 'I knew I wouldn't like her! She's sent my trunk away.'

'I'm really very sorry,' apologized Gran. 'But not to worry, we'll just have to get it back.'

'Not a moment to lose,' shouted the vampire. 'That trunk is very, very precious. I can't have it shunted all over the place, just because you forgot that I even existed.'

'You're quite right,' agreed Gran. 'I'll just phone the company and explain the mistake and see if they can bring the trunk back.'

'They better had,' snapped Vlad. 'And fast, too, or

it's vampirising time.'

So Gran phoned up and the company said the trunk had come back to the warehouse and they were going to keep it there all night.

Vlad stood on the telephone and shook his head vigorously.

'Tell them no,' he said urgently. 'Tell them definitely no. Tell them we'll come and fetch it right now.'

So Gran took the address of the warehouse and they set off in her car to rescue the lost trunk.

On the way Paul asked, 'Whatever have you got in that trunk that is so important?'

'Never you mind,' replied Vlad rudely. 'That trunk is my very own private business and when I finally get it I shall put it in the cellar and no one, absolutely no one, is to touch it. Anyone who does will get very badly vampirized, and don't you forget it.'

'I think you're behaving very badly about this trunk,' said Judy angrily.

Vlad burst into tears. 'You're all ganging up on me. I only came over to help with the snoglet and you're all ganging up on me. Poor Old Vlad, Poor Little Drac.'

'Poor Vlad,' said Gran sympathetically. 'I expect

he's tired after his long flight and he's upset about his lost trunk.'

'No, it's not that,' explained Paul. 'He's always like that, he's always sorry for himself. I think he enjoys it.'

'I don't,' yelled Vlad. 'It's just that you're all so horrible to me.'

To Gran's relief they saw the warehouse ahead. They parked the car and walked up the metal staircase into the dark, red-brick building. Gran knocked on the window of the Enquiries Section. A man opened it and asked, 'Can I help you, madam?'

Vlad flew on to the desk.

'No, you can't help her,' he told the amazed man. 'But you can help me. It's *my* trunk you ran off with. Now get it out and look sharp about it.'

'What's going on around here?' asked the warehouse man, scratching his head. 'Who is this, anyway?'

Vlad tapped his foot on the counter with irritation.

'I, sir, am Vlad the Drac, Mr V. Drac to you, and you have my trunk.'

Gran coughed quietly.

'I'm afraid it's all my fault,' she explained. 'You see,

your men delivered Mr Drac's trunk but I didn't know he was staying with my son and I sent it back.'

'Just one moment,' said the warehouse man, 'and I'll look into it.'

The man had only been gone a minute when Vlad began to worry.

'He's taking his time. I expect they've lost my trunk. I'll never see it again and it's all your fault,' he told Gran.

'You worry too much, dear,' Gran told the vampire.' He'll be back in a minute with your trunk.'

'He better had,' growled Vlad.
Fortunately a moment or two later the man returned to say they had found the trunk and would deliver it the next day.

'That won't do,' yelled Vlad. 'I've got to have it today. We'll take it in the car.'

'But it's too big,' exclaimed Paul, looking at the trunk.

'It looks like a coffin,' commented Judy. 'It gives me the creeps.'

'Don't be ridiculous,' said Vlad. 'It's nothing like a coffin; you've been reading too many vampire books. It's nothing like a coffin and we can easily strap it on the top of the car.'

So two of the men carried the trunk out and put it on the roof of Gran's car and tied it on firmly. Vlad was much more cheerful after that and waved from the car window as they drove off.

When they got home Dad was waiting for them.

'Wherever have you been?' he asked, kissing Gran on the cheek. 'We were waiting at the hospital.'

'We had to go and fetch Vlad's trunk, dear,' Gran told Dad. 'Could you help us get it down off the car roof?'

Dad looked uneasily at the trunk.

'Where do you think you're going to keep this thing?' Dad asked Vlad.

'The cellar will do very nicely,' Vlad told him.

So Dad and Paul and Judy lifted the trunk down from the car roof. Dad put it down and mopped his brow.

'It weighs a ton. What have you got in there, a body?'

'If you ask a silly question, you can expect a silly answer,' snapped Vlad. 'Now, will you please carry it carefully down into the cellar without any further fuss.'

So Dad and the children carried the trunk down the steep cellar stairs. Vlad flew on ahead and put

the light on and proceeded to give instructions.

'Careful, careful, don't bump against the side, easy, easy, over to the left a bit, that's right, whoa, gently does it.'

Eventually the precious trunk lay on the cellar floor.

'Judy's quite right,' commented Dad. 'It really does look like a coffin.'

'You're only saying that 'cos I'm a vampire,' complained Vlad. 'If it was any old person's trunk you wouldn't even think of it. Poor Old Vlad, Poor Little Drac.'

'He's off,' said Dad. 'Let's get out of here before he starts.'

So they all left the cellar and went to have the supper that Gran had brought with her. Gran laid a special place for Vlad with a tin of green shoe polish just for him. Vlad was delighted.

'Just the same colour as me,' he told Gran, beaming broadly. 'It's a perfect match, you are clever. She's not bad, your mum,' he told Dad.

'I'll drink to that,' said Dad. 'In fact, I think I should open a bottle of wine and we can drink a toast to Gran and wet the baby's head.'

'Wet the baby's head?' exclaimed Vlad in horror. 'Why should you want to do that to the poor little thing? Honestly, the things people think of! No vampire would ever want to wet a new-born baby's head.'

'It's an expression, Vlad,' Judy explained. 'It means drinking a toast to the baby and wishing her health and long life and things.'

'Oh,' said Vlad. 'Well, that's all right, I suppose, though why people can't say what they mean I shall never know.'

Dad went off to get the wine and returned a moment later.

'Someone's locked the cellar door,' he complained. 'Who's got the key?'

'Me,' said Vlad. 'And I shall keep it. Anyone who wants to go down to that cellar will have to ask me and be accompanied.'

'Don't be ridiculous,' shouted Dad. 'It's my cellar and I will go into it whenever I want to.'

'It's my trunk down there,' replied Vlad. 'And I don't want anyone interfering with it.'

'Why should anyone interfere with it?' demanded Dad.

'I don't know,' said Vlad. 'But people are very odd, they do funny things.'

Judy looked at Gran and Gran looked at Paul.

'I've never seen your cellar, dear,' said Gran to Dad. 'If Vlad would give me the key I could go and choose a nice bottle of wine to wet the baby's head with.'

'Well, all right,' said Vlad. 'I'll come and help you.'

'What on earth do you think he's got in that trunk?' asked Dad while they were gone.

'Maybe it's Great Uncle Ghitza,' said Judy, giggling.

'Maybe it's Count Dracula,' suggested Paul.

'Maybe you two have big imaginations,' laughed Dad.

Vlad and Gran returned with a bottle of wine. When it was poured Vlad lifted his egg cup and said, 'Ladies and Gentlemen, I give you Gran and Zoë Louise Snoglet Vladivostock Stone.'

3

The Chamber of Horrors

The next day the whole family sat round Mum's bed admiring the baby. Gran was delighted with her new grandchild. Vlad disappeared to visit some friends he had made at the hospital during Paul's stay there.

'Now, listen, you two,' said Mum to Judy and Paul. 'You've got to get Vlad out of the house. It's not a good idea for Dad and Vlad to be in the house at the same time, especially without me to keep the peace.'

'Gran's doing very well,' Paul assured her.

'I'm sure she is,' said Mum. 'But it's a bit much to expect her to do it all the time. So you two will have to take a couple of days off school and I want you to take Vlad out a lot and show him London and keep him out of Dad's way as much as you can.'

'Oh Mum,' groaned Judy. 'That means we won't be able to come and see you and Vladivostock, I mean Zoë Louise, very much.'

'I know,' agreed Mum. 'But I won't be in hospital long and you will be able to see her every day once I'm home.'

'All right,' agreed Paul. 'We'll do it.'

'Thanks,' said Mum gratefully. 'Now, here's £20; that should cover fares and food for a couple of days.'

When Vlad came back the children told him that they were going to show him London.

'Good idea,' agreed the vampire. 'This is my fourth visit to London; it's about time I got to know the place.'

'Where would you like to go?' asked Mum.

'I would like to see the Tower of London,' announced the vampire.

'Good idea,' said Judy.

'I'd like that, too,' agreed Paul.

'I wonder if I'll meet Great Uncle Ghitza there,' pondered the vampire.

'Why should you expect to meet *him* there?' asked Judy in amazement.

''Cos there's a Bloody Tower there,' explained Vlad. 'And that's just the kind of place you'd expect to meet vampires – particularly the Great Uncle Ghitza type of vampire.'

'I think it's called the Bloody Tower because lots

of people had their heads chopped off there,' said Paul.

'I don't know,' sighed Vlad. 'People go on about vampires but I never heard of a vampire cutting off people's heads.'

So the next day the children and Vlad left the house and got into the queue to wait for a bus. They waited for a long time and then a bus that was full up went straight by.

'That bus didn't even stop,' complained Vlad. 'The driver must have seen us standing here freezing to death and he didn't even stop.'

'Be quiet, Vlad,' said Judy. 'Everyone's looking at us.'

'Are they?' said Vlad, brightening up. 'Jolly good.' And standing on Paul's shoulder he harangued the queue.

'It's a disgrace, that's what it is. The next bus that comes by had better stop or there'll be some vampirising done.'

At first the people in the queue were a bit surprised to be addressed by a small angry green vampire. Then someone piped up: 'You're Vlad the Drac, aren't you?'

'I most certainly am,' replied the vampire. 'Would

you like my autograph?'

Soon everyone in the queue was chatting away and agreeing that the service was very bad.

'Right,' said Vlad. 'Action is required and who better than a vampire to take it?'

'Whatever it is that you're planning, Vlad,' said Paul, 'please forget it.'

'Certainly not,' replied the vampire indignantly. 'I'm having a good time.'

'Grab him, Judy,' yelled Paul. 'He's going to get us into trouble.'

But it was too late. Vlad flew off and sat on a woman's shoulder and got a piece of paper and a pencil from her.

'Now where are you going, love?' he asked the first person in the queue. 'Oxford Street, right, and you, sir? Knightsbridge, good.'

Soon Vlad had a list of the destinations of everyone in the queue. When Vlad had finished he flew back to Judy and sat on her shoulder.

'What are you planning, Vlad?' she asked anxiously.

'I am going to hijack the bus,' explained the vampire.

'I don't understand,' said Judy faintly.

'You will,' Vlad assured her. 'You will.'

37

As the bus came into sight Vlad addressed the queue.

'All right, troops, when the bus stops everyone pile on and leave the rest to me.'

So when the bus stopped everyone paid their fare to the driver and went and sat down.

'We're to get on last,' Vlad told the children. So feeling very uneasy Judy and Paul clambered on to the bus aftereveryone else.

'Two halves to the Tower of London, please,' said Vlad pleasantly.

'This bus doesn't go to the Tower of London,' said the bus driver.

'Oh yes, it does,' Vlad told him. 'This is a hijack. This bus is going to the Tower of London via Oxford Street, Knightsbridge, The Houses of Parliament and Paddington Station.'

'But that's all over London,' protested the bus driver. ' It will take all morning. I won't do it.'

Vlad flew over and sat on the driver's shoulder.

'Oh, I think you will,' he said, 'or I'll vampirise you on the spot.'

'You wouldn't,' said the bus driver. 'You're bluffing. You're Vlad the Drac. You're a vegetarian.'

'Not on Tuesday mornings,' replied Vlad, clacking

his teeth and baring his fangs. 'Want me to prove it?'

'No, no,' yelled the bus driver. 'Anything but that. I suppose I'll have to do what you want. All right, where do I go first?'

'The lady with the two small children first, I think. Oxford Street, am I right, madam?'

'That's right, Vlad,' she replied.

'Okay everyone, hang on to your hats, Oxford Street first stop.'

Everyone cheered and shouted, 'Good Old Vlad.'

So the bus went all over London, dropping people off where they wanted. Everyone was grateful to Vlad and said they wished he was around more often.

Eventually they got to the Tower of London. Judy and Paul apologized to the driver who said that he'd had a very interesting morning.

'Makes a change you know, not always going on the same route. Something to tell the kids, too, how I got hijacked by a vampire. Yeah, man, how I got hijacked by a vampire and escaped with my life and blood.'

'You were very brave,' Vlad assured him. 'I really was in a vampirising mood.'

'It makes my blood run cold to think of it.' said the bus driver shivering, and he drove off as Paul and Judy and Vlad stood and waved him goodbye.

'I enjoyed that,' said Vlad. 'That was good.'
'You were jolly lucky he believed you,' said Judy. 'And you are to promise never, ever to do that again.'

'Not fair,' grumbled the vampire. 'I was only helping people. Poor Old Vlad, Poor Little Drac.'

'Never mind that,' said Judy. 'You promise to behave or we won't take you into the Tower of London.'

'All right,' conceded the vampire reluctantly. "Cos I really do want to see the Bloody Tower in case there really are some vampires there.'

So Judy and Paul joined the queue to go in; Vlad hopped into Judy's pocket so that she wouldn't have to pay for him too. They looked around the Tower; Vlad liked the towering white turrets and big court-yards.

'It reminds me of home,' he said wistfully. 'Just the sort of place a vampire likes.'

Eventually they came to the Bloody Tower. They joined a group of tourists being shown round by a guide. Everyone stood round the guide listening quietly to all the information about the Tower. Vlad listened impatiently for a minute or two and then said in a loud voice, 'No vampires anywhere, not one single vampire.'

The guide coughed, glared at Vlad and went on:

'And it was in this very room that Anne Boleyn was told that she would be beheaded. It is said that her headless ghost haunts the tower.'

'A headless ghost,' shrieked Vlad. 'Let me out of here!'

Vlad flew off Judy's shoulder, flapped around a bit and disappeared. Judy and Paul crept around the room looking for him, trying very hard to be quiet, while the guide droned on. 'Vlad, where are you?' whispered Judy.

'Vlad,' called Paul quietly. 'Wherever you are, come out.'

As Paul came near to a suit of armour standing stiff and gleaming on a pedestal, he heard a muffled sound.

'Judy,' whispered Paul. 'I think he's inside the suit of armour.'

Suddenly the suit of armour crashed to the floor with a terrible noise, making the group of tourists start.

'It's the ghost,' screamed a woman.

'It's Anne Boleyn,' shrieked someone else.

'I'm getting out of here,' said a third and they all rushed out screaming with the guide following, calling, 'Come back, come back.'

Judy and Paul were left alone with the fallen suit of armour.

'Vlad,' said Paul sternly. 'Where are you?'

'In here,' came a muffled voice. 'Get me out.'

Eventually Paul pulled back the visor on the helmet and out flew Vlad.

'How did you do that?' asked Judy.

'I don't know,' said Vlad. 'I flew into the armour to hide from the ghost without a head and that thing came down and I was trapped and then the whole thing fell over. It gave me quite a shock, I can tell you.'

Judy giggled.

'All the tourists thought you were the ghost and ran away,' she told Vlad.

Vlad grinned. 'Almost as good as vampirising 'em,' he said.

'What shall we do now?' asked Judy.

'Let's go to the Chamber of Horrors,' suggested Vlad. 'We might find some vampires there.'

'I'm tired,' said Paul. 'Let's just go home.'

'That's what I'd like, too,' agreed Judy.

'Nonsense, nonsense,' said Vlad. 'The day is young. Now, it says here in my Guide Book that Madame Tussaud's waxworks, including the Chamber of Horrors, is in Baker Street. So which bus should we take?'

Paul and Judy looked at each other.

'No more buses, Vlad,' said Paul firmly. 'Absolutely not, even if we have to walk home. I couldn't face another trip like that last one.'

'Me neither,' agreed Judy, shuddering.

'What are you two on about?' said Vlad indignantly. 'I didn't do anything.'

'We'll go on the tube,' said Judy. 'You'll like that, Vlad.'

'The tube?' asked the vampire suspiciously. 'What is it?'

'It's trains that go underground,' she told him. 'Come on, you'll see.'

So the children bought two tickets and went down the escalator to the platform where the trains came in.

'Ha,' said Vlad approvingly. 'Down into the bowels of the earth. Just the sort of place vampires like.'

'You won't find many vampires down here,' Paul told him.

'You'd be surprised,' said Vlad. 'I'm telling you, you would be surprised.'

A train came rattling into the station, the doors opened and they got on. The two children went and sat down and Vlad went and hung by his feet from one of the straps that hung from the ceiling of the train.

'What's this for really?' asked Vlad, from his upside-down position.

'It's for people to strap-hang from when the trains are full,' Judy told him.

'I don't quite follow you, dear girl,' said Vlad, swinging from one foot.

'I'll show you,' said Paul and standing on tip-toe he grasped the strap next to Vlad.

'You see, if I hang on to this I won't fall over when the train stops.'

'Well, no one had better try to hang on to *this* strap,' said Vlad fiercely. 'This strap is mine.'

Judy and Paul felt uneasy as the train filled up and soon all the seats were taken and people began to hang on to the straps. At the station before Baker Street lots of people got on the train.

'Thank goodness it's only one more stop,' said Judy.

A man with a briefcase grabbed hold of Vlad's strap.

'You let go this minute,' snapped the vampire, 'or I'll vampirise you on the spot.'

The man dropped his briefcase on Paul's toe.

'Ouch,' yelled Paul.

'Sorry,' said the man. 'But what's going on?'

'That's Vlad the Drac, he's staying with us,' explained Judy. 'And we had to take him out to keep him out of Dad's hair and he hijacked a bus, so we're taking him to the Chamber of Horrors by train.'

'Oh,' said the man, looking confused. 'Do you think you're allowed to bring a vampire on the tube? I mean, he's very aggressive and he could sit on your knee; he doesn't need a strap all to himself.'

'Oh yes I do.' said Vlad. 'And you are a very greedy person and richly deserve vampirising,' and Vlad clacked his teeth at the man.

'Pull the communication cord,' yelled the man. 'Stop the train immediately! There's a dangerous vampire on board!'

At that moment the train drew into Baker Street station.

'Run for it,' yelled Paul, shoving Vlad into his pocket and grabbing Judy's hand.

They pushed their way off the train and ran along the platform and up some stairs, followed by the man, shouting, 'Stop that vampire!'

The children ran through the barrier and out into the street and hid behind a newspaper stall. After a while the row seemed to have died down and Judy and Paul crept out.

'Whew,' said Paul. 'That was a near thing. Come on, let's go home.'

'Not before I've seen the Chamber of Horrors,' declared Vlad.

'You don't deserve any more treats,' said Judy. 'You've been so awful.'

'Nonsense,' said Vlad. 'All I did was assert my right to a strap and people go barmy. Poor Old Vlad, Poor Little Drac.'

So reluctantly the children walked to the waxworks and bought the tickets they needed.

'You do realize that it's almost closing time, love?' said the woman at the counter. 'You'll only have just over half an hour.'

'That's quite enough time for me to find out if there are any vampires in the Chamber of Horrors,' declared Vlad.

They went into the waxworks and Vlad flew over to a policeman.

'Pardon me, sir, but could you direct me to the Chamber of Horrors?'

There was no answer. Vlad got cross.

'What's the matter with you?' he yelled indignantly.' 'Can't you give a civil answer to a civil question?'

There was still no answer.

'Right,' exclaimed Vlad. 'It's time you were taught a lesson,' and he sank his teeth into the policeman's neck. There was still no response, then Vlad let out a shriek.

'It's not a person, it's wax! Ugggg! It tastes horrible.'

'Yes, well, you're in the waxworks,' said Judy. 'It's where you wanted to go.'

'Yes, well, let's get to the Chamber of Horrors,' said the vampire, wiping the wax from his teeth, 'and stop all this messing around.'

Eventually they found their way down to the Chamber of Horrors.

'You've only got a few minutes,' said the guard.

'Any vampires in there?' asked Vlad hopefully. 'Like my Great Uncle Ghitza, for instance?'

'Not that I've noticed,' said the guard.

'In that case,' announced Vlad, 'your collection of horrors is very inadequate, uncomprehensive and incomplete. Lead on, Judith, take me into this famous chamber.'

Vlad was very disappointed to find no vampires.

'Not much of a place,' he complained. 'Not worth coming to, really. I think I'll go to sleep,' and yawning he climbed into Judy's pocket.

'Thank God for that,' said Paul. 'Hopefully he'll stay asleep until we get home. Come on, let's go.'

So the children ran out and went home as fast as they could. When they got back they told Dad and

Gran all about the day.

'He's a monster,' declared Dad. 'I don't know why we put up with him.'

'Quietly, dear,' said Gran. 'He might hear you.'

'I don't care if he does,' announced Dad.

Judy peeped in her pocket to see if Vlad had woken up.

'He's not there,' she said. 'Have you got him, Paul?'

Paul looked. 'No, he's not on me,' he said.

'He must have climbed out.' said Judy in dismay. 'Oh no, we must have left him behind in the Chamber of Horrors.'

4

The Blood Transfusion

Dad was delighted when he heard that Vlad was in the Chamber of Horrors.

'Ha!' he shouted. 'And a very good place for him. He'll fit in beautifully. Now, why didn't I think of that before?'

'Oh, Dad,' responded Judy. 'Don't be so rotten. Poor little Vlad. He'll be so scared. You've got to get him out.'

'What do you expect me to do?' demanded Dad. 'Madame Tussaud's is closed till the morning and even for you I am not prepared to break into a public building.'

'There must be someone on duty all night,' insisted Judy. 'You could phone them up.'

'Phone them up!' exclaimed Dad. 'What do you expect me to say? I'm sorry, I know this sounds a little odd, but our vampire escaped from my daughter's pocket and is somewhere in the Chamber of Horrors. We think he may be a bit scared and we'd like you to go and look for him.'

'Well, yes,' said Judy. 'Something like that.'

'Well, I won't,' said Dad. 'And that's that.'

'Oh, Dad,' sniffed Judy.

'They wouldn't listen,' continued Dad. 'They'd think I was a nutter and hang up on me.'

'But, Dad,' intervened Paul, 'we can't just leave him there.'

'*I* can,' said Dad. 'Easily'.

'No, Nick,' said Gran. 'The children are quite right, it's not fair to poor Vlad. I'll give them a ring and explain.'

'Thanks, Gran,' said the children.

'My own mother,' said Dad, 'and even she isn't on my side.'

So Gran went and phoned up the waxworks and explained what had happened. After a while she put the phone down.

'They've gone to look and they're going to phone us back,' she told Judy and Paul.

'Oh, poor Vlad,' said Judy on the verge of tears. 'I hope he hasn't woken up yet, then he won't have had a chance to get scared.'

'Oh yes,' agreed Dad. 'Poor Old Vlad, Poor Little

Drac. Locked up with a whole lot of horrible waxworks. Still, I bet none of them are as horrible as
him. It's probably those unfortunate waxworks that
are having a hard time.'

'Oh Dad,' wept Judy. 'You are being awful.'

At that moment the phone rang.

Gran picked it up.

'You've found him. Oh, well done, and what a relief.
Oh dear, he's fainted. Yes, I suppose hospital would be
the best thing. I don't know, just a moment, I'll ask.'

Gran turned to the family. 'They've found him,'
she said. 'He's just fainted and he muttered "television" just before he passed out. They want to know
if you know what he meant.'

'Publicity,' shouted Dad. 'That's what he wants. It's
all a publicity stunt. Get the TV cameras there. Vlad
the Drac is back in town, folks.'

'What do you think?' Gran asked Judy and Paul.

'I think Dad's right,' Judy admitted reluctantly.

'Yes,' sighed Paul 'He may not have got himself
locked in on purpose but he couldn't let the chance
of a bit of publicity pass him by.'

'I see,' said Gran and she picked up the phone again.

'I gather that Vlad would like the press and media
informed,' she told them. 'Oh good, well, that's fine

for everyone then. All's well that ends well. Thank you so much. Yes, we'll come and fetch him from the hospital tomorrow. Goodnight.'

'Well?' asked Judy.

'Madame Tussaud's are pleased at the idea of a little publicity too and they're dealing with all of that and then Vlad will go the hospital for the night.'

'Poor Vlad,' said Judy. 'I hope he really is all right.'

'Poor Vlad!' exploded Dad. 'I expect he's having the time of his life, in the headlines once again, and meanwhile I've got two sets of hospitals to visit. Poor Old Dad, Poor Little Nick.'

However, the next day Dad did agree to take the children and Gran to the hospital to collect Vlad, although he complained bitterly.

'I don't see how I can be expected to do everything,' he moaned. 'Look after your mother and the two of you, run round after Vlad and, on top of all of that, there's a meat thief in the house.'

'A what?' asked Gran and the children.

'A meat thief,' repeated Dad. 'As soon as I put a bit of meat in the fridge it disappears.'

'Very odd,' commented Gran, as they drove into the hospital car park, Dad went up to the information desk.

'I'm looking for, er, Vlad the Drac,' he said sheepishly.

'Who?' asked the man at the desk.

'Vlad the Drac,' repeated Dad and, lowering his voice, said, 'He's a vampire.'

'Oh, the vampire!' said the man, lowering his voice too. 'We put him in a private room, so as not to scare the other patients. You'll find him in room 115a on the third floor.'

The Stones went up in the big hospital lift to the third floor. Judy ran out of the lift and raced to room 115a and burst in. There in a huge bed lay Vlad, not moving at all.

'Vlad,' shrieked Judy. 'Say something. Speak to me.'

Vlad didn't move and as the others came in Judy burst into tears.

'He wasn't pretending,' she told them. 'He's had such a shock that he can't move and it's all our fault.'

While she was speaking a doctor came in.

'Mr Stone?' she asked.

'That's me,' admitted Dad.

'I gather the – er – patient is staying with you at present.'

'That's right,' agreed Dad.

'Is he going to be all right?' demanded Judy.

'Poor old Vlad,' commented Paul. 'He does look very small lying there. He will recover, won't he?'

'Well, it's hard for me to judge,' explained the doctor. 'I've never had to deal with a vampire before. But maybe we could talk about this outside, just in case he can hear what we're saying.'

So they all went out of the room, Dad leading a shaken Paul and Gran comforting the weeping Judy.

'All right, Doctor,' said Dad. 'Tell us the truth, we can take it. Is he going to be all right?'

'As far as I can tell,' replied the doctor, 'there's nothing wrong with him. He just lies there moaning "television" from time to time. Now, I believe Vlad likes getting a lot of publicity. Is that right?'

'That's right,' confirmed Dad. 'He does indeed.'

'Well, I think this illness is all a sham to get publicity. I think he's as fit as you and I, but what we're going to do about it I don't know.'

'I do,' said Judy, drying her tears.

'Thought you were on his side,' commented Dad.

'I am,' said Judy. 'But I think we need to know if he's pretending or if he's really ill. If he's play-acting he deserves to be taught a lesson and if he's really ill then he must stay in hospital.'

'So what do you want us to do?' asked the doctor.

'I'm intrigued.'

'You should suggest that Vlad has a blood transfusion,' Judy told her.

'But, Judy dear,' said Gran, 'poor Vlad faints at the sight of blood.'

'Exactly,' said Judy. 'So the plan is a nurse goes in and opens the window. Then we go in and all talk about blood transfusions. Then we all go out again while the nurse fetches the blood. If Vlad is pretending, he can fly out of the window, and if he isn't then at least we'll know what's going on.'

'Brilliant,' said Dad.

'Foolproof,' agreed Paul.

'Cunning,' recommended Gran.

'You're quite a psychologist, young lady,' said the doctor admiringly. 'Right, let's get going.'

So the nurse went in and opened the window. As she left, the doctor and the Stones walked in.

The nurse winked at them.

'Shall I get the equipment ready, Doctor?' she asked.

'Please, nurse,' said the doctor. 'And tell the anaesthetist to be ready, just in case.'

Vlad blinked.

'So you think a blood transfusion is the only way then, Doctor?' said Dad in a loud voice.

'Oh, *no*,' shrieked Judy 'You can't give poor Vlad a *blood* transfusion.'

'He'd hate it,' agreed Paul. 'I can't think of anything Vlad would hate more than a *blood* transfusion.'

'Now, now,' said Gran comfortingly. 'Sometimes a blood transfusion is a good thing and it doesn't hurt.'

'Well, I'm not going to stay here to watch,' sobbed Judy. 'Dad, I want to go home.'

'All right, dear,' said Dad. 'Don't take on. I'll take you home. Come on, Paul and Gran, help me get Judy home. Doctor, do what you must, and good luck.'

With one last look at Vlad the Stones left.

'Alright, nurse,' called the doctor. 'We're ready for the blood transfusion in room 115a. I'll come and help you with the equipment.'

As the Stones walked out of the hospital into the car park, Judy felt a familiar touch on her shoulder.

'Vlad,' she said, trying not to laugh. 'The blood transfusion helped.'

'Don't be ridiculous,' he replied. 'I just got better very suddenly and I don't want to talk about it and I never, ever want to go to hospital again.'

Later that day the Stones went to visit Mum and the baby. Vlad insisted that he was too shocked to go visiting and that he would be fine if they left him at home on his own. When they got back Vlad was nowhere to be found.

'Vlad,' called Judy. 'Vlad, where are you?'

A moment later Vlad emerged from the cellar.

'What's the problem?' he asked.

'There isn't a problem,' said Judy. 'I just wondered where you were.'

'I was down in the cellar checking my trunk,' said the vampire.

'What's in that trunk?' asked Judy.

'It's my secret,' Vlad told her. 'It's my little secret and I'm not going to tell you, so there.'

At that moment there was a shriek from Dad.

'The meat has gone again. I left pork chops in here for supper and they've gone. Vlad, do you know anything about this?'

Vlad flew into the kitchen.

'What would I want with meat? A vegetarian like me? You just like to blame everything on me. Even though I've been through a trauma, you still think that everything that goes wrong is my fault. Poor Old Vlad, Poor Little Drac.'

'I only asked,' said Dad.

Just then the front door bell rang.

Paul went and answered it and there on the doorstep stood P. C. Wiggins.

'Hello, Paul,' said P. C. Wiggins. 'I'm afraid I've come to see Vlad. I have reason to think that he's staying with you again.'

'You'd better come in,' said Paul.

Vlad flew over and sat on P. C. Wiggins' shoulder.

'Hello, P. C. Wiggins,' he called. 'How delightful to see you. Did I hear you were looking for me? Is it to do with my night of horror in the Chamber of Horrors?'

'Well, er, no,' replied the policeman.

'Oh, I see,' said Vlad, smiling cheerfully. 'So it's just a social call to say hello to an old friend. How very civil. And how are you these days, P.C. Wiggins?'

'Oh, not so bad, thank you,' replied the policeman. 'Mustn't grumble, you know.'

'Mustn't grumble!' exclaimed Vlad in amazement.' Mustn't grumble – whatever do you mean?'

The policeman looked a bit surprised and coughed in embarrassment. 'You know, mustn't grumble – can't complain, like.'

'Mustn't grumble, can't complain!' exclaimed the vampire in disgust. 'You must be barmy. I mean, you could be saying "Poor Old P. C., Poor Little Wiggins" all the time if you wanted to.'

'Well, eh, yes,' said the policeman, coughing again. 'I think I'll pass on that one if you don't mind. Now, I'm here, Vlad, because the butcher tells me that you've been seen stealing meat from his shop.'

'That's silly,' said Vlad, looking at his feet. 'Why should a vegetarian steal meat?'

'That's what I thought,' agreed the policeman. 'But there are lots of witnesses. Six people saw you fly away with a big piece of sirloin steak from Mr Garupa's shop. Now, come on Vlad, own up and tell us why you did it.'

'Yes,' said Judy. 'Have you stopped being a vegetarian or something?'

'Did you take it for us?' quizzed Dad. 'And forgot to hand it over?'

'I did take the meat,' confessed the vampire. 'I

remember now. I must have been in a state of shock after my terrible experiences. A night alone in the Chamber of Horrors does odd things to the mind. Yes, I remember now, I did have this strange urge to steal meat.'

'Well,' declared Dad. 'I don't understand this at all and I refuse to accept any responsibility for what this vampire gets up to. He is merely a temporary, very temporary, resident in my home.'

'Well,' said P. C. Wiggins, taking off his hat, 'I don't know what to do. Mr Garupa said that he wouldn't prosecute if you promised never to do it again. Are you prepared to give that promise, Vlad?'

'I promise,' said Vlad. 'On my oath as a vampire, on Great Uncle Ghitza's fangs, on Aunt Olga's saucepan, on Grandfather Anatoly's books, on Count Dracula's coffin, on my poor dear mother's . . .'

'Stop,' yelled Dad. 'Just promise never to do it again.'

'That's just what I was about to do,' said Vlad indignantly. 'On Great Uncle Ghitza's . . .'

P. C. Wiggins coughed. 'Yes, well, I've got all that in my notebook. Now, just promise.'

Vlad continued, 'I will never, never, under any circumstances steal meat again from Mr Garupa's shop.'

'Or any other shop,' continued P. C. Wiggins.

'You mean, I've got to promise never to steal meat from anywhere ever again?'

'Of course,' said the policeman. 'If you don't, we'll have to bring a charge against you for theft.'

'It's not fair,' moaned Vlad. 'People ask too much. Poor Old Vlad, Poor Little Drac.'

'But, Vlad, what would you want meat for?' demanded Paul.

'I just want to be free to do what I want,' complained the vampire, 'and not have people saying don't do this and don't do that or else.'

'Well, you can't go around stealing things,' said Dad fiercely. 'And if you do, you'll regret it. Swatting is nothing compared to what I'll do if I hear any more of this. Now, do you promise?'

'Oh, all right,' groaned the vampire and they all joined in the refrain of 'Poor Old Vlad, Poor Little Drac'.

Later that evening as Judy took Vlad up to bed, Vlad commented to her, 'Did you hear P .C. Wiggins saying all that nonsense about "Can't complain" and "Mustn't grumble"? I'm shocked, Judy, deeply shocked. That's the trouble with people: they just don't know how to enjoy themselves. Just think how many "Poor Old P. C., Poor Little Wigginses" he has missed out on (and out of choice) in his life. It doesn't bear thinking about. You know, Judy, if I live to be a thousand years old, I shall never, never, never understand people.'

5
The B~~~~ Good Show

The following afternoon Dad and the children went off to see Mum. Vlad said that he felt much too ill to go out and stayed at home with Gran to keep an eye on him.

The phone rang and Gran answered it.

'It's for you, Vlad,' she called.

'I can't talk to anyone,' he said dramatically. 'I've been through a terrible experience and I'm too ill.'

'It's Barry Slogan,' Gran told him.

'Never met anyone with that name in my life,' said the vampire. 'Say I'm not in.'

'He has a television chat show,' Gran told the vampire.

Vlad leapt up.

'Television! Why didn't you say so?' And he flew over to the phone and grabbed the receiver.

'Hiya, Bas, how you doing? Vlad the Drac here. What's that? The Chamber of Horrors, yes, it's true. I had a harrowing experience, harrowing, I can tell you. Tell the nation? On your programme? Tonight? Just a minute while I check my busy little diary. Well, I do have two very important arrangements but for you I'll break them. Tonight then, it will be a pleasure. No, not at all, I'm not too ill. I owe it to the people of this country to tell them about my experience, it's the least I can do. You'll send a car at seven then, splendid. See you later, bye now, Bas.'

'Ha,' said Vlad to Gran. 'Fancy that. Barry Slogan wants me on his chat show. My night in the Chamber of Horrors wasn't wasted, after all.'

'That's wonderful, Vlad,' answered Gran. 'I'm proud of you. Now, up you go and put on your best suit ready for the car from the television studios.'

'Umm,' said Vlad. 'Of course, I do want to look my best on television but on the other hand I've just been through a traumatic and devastating experience – I've got to talk about My Night in the Chamber of Horrors. I must look exhausted, haunted, haggard, troubled and distraught.'

'How are you going to do that?' asked Gran.

'Like this,' said the vampire and he undid his shirt, threw away his tie, ruffled his hair and sat with his forehead resting on his hand.

'How do I look?' he asked Gran. 'Would you think I'd been through a night of unprecedented travail – if you didn't know, that is?'

'Oh, I would,' said Gran. 'You look terrible, I mean just as if you'd had a really bad time.'

About an hour later the doorbell rang. Gran answered.

'Car for Mr Vlad the Drac,' said the chauffeur.

'I'll get him,' said Gran.

'Carry me out on the cushion,' said Vlad. 'As though I were an invalid.'

So Gran did and handed the cushion to the chauffeur.

'Is that him?' asked the chauffeur in disgust. 'I'm not taking him, not without danger money.'

'He's quite harmless,' Gran assured him. 'A vegetarian, you know.'

'That's as may be,' replied the chauffeur, 'but he looks like a lot of trouble to me and I don't want to be alone with him in the back of my car and that's that.'

'I'll come with you, then,' said Gran brightly. 'It will be an adventure. Just give me five minutes. I'll have to leave a note, wash my hands and then I'll be with you.'

'Right you are, missus,' said the chauffeur, gingerly taking the cushion from Gran and giving Vlad an old-fashioned look. As soon as Gran had gone the chauffeur said fiercely, 'You'd better behave or it's garlic for you — I know how to deal with vampires.'

Vlad looked up from his cushion.

'You don't look worth vampirising to me,' he said languidly.

'Don't give me that,' said the chauffeur. 'I know all about vampires. I never miss a film about vampires. I know why you're weak. Because it's not yet really dark. Vampires can't bear the light; as soon as it's really pitch black out there, you'll be at my throat. Don't deny it.'

'But I'm not like that,' said Vlad, sitting up indignantly. 'I'd like to be but I'm a vegetarian, unfortunately.'

'Oh, yeah,' sneered the chauffeur.

'Yes,' insisted Vlad. 'I faint just at the sight of blood. My son Ghitza is quite different but me, alas, I'm harmless.'

'Oh, very clever,' insisted the chauffeur. 'You won't kid me that easily; you just want me to relax and feel safe so that it's easier for you to suck my blood —

well, I've got news for you, mate, I'm not as daft as you think. You can sit in the back of my car with that lady and I'm going to keep the glass window between me and the passengers shut all the way and don't you start thinking any different.'

Vlad's eyes began to gleam as he saw a chance to really scare someone. He lay back on his pillow.

'The light,' he cried, putting his hand in front of his eyes. 'Let the light vanish – the eye of the vampire cannot suffer light.' He sat up on his elbow. 'The light begins to fade, the appetite of the vampire demands blood, human blood. I crave the blood of the nearest human.'

The chauffeur dropped Vlad and the cushion, jumped into his car, closed all the windows tight and drove off. When Gran came out she found Vlad lying on the pavement roaring with laughter.

'What happened?' she asked.

'As the light fades from the night sky the vampire demands blood,' Vlad explained, giggling.

'You scared that poor man,' said Gran sternly.

'Not really,' confessed Vlad. 'He scared himself. He goes to too many horror films.'

'Oh, well,' said Gran. 'Silly man. We'll have to go in my car, then.'

When Dad, Paul and Judy got home they found Gran's note.

'Vlad and Gran have gone to the Television Centre, so that Vlad can be on the Barry Slogan Show,' Dad told the children.

Paul grabbed a newspaper.

'It's on in five minutes,' he yelled. 'Come on.' So soon they were all sitting in front of the television eating TV dinners.

'Poor Barry Slogan,' commented Dad. 'I bet Vlad will manage to shake his suave exterior. He won't be able to go on smiling through this one.'

The first guest wasn't Vlad and the Stones sat waiting patiently for the vampire's turn. After a while

The ⭐ BARRY ⭐ SLOGAN SHOW

GUEST STAR VLAD THE DRAC

Barry Slogan turned to the camera and said, 'And now, ladies and gentlemen, my next guest is someone, if someone is the right word, whom you will all have heard of. Now, I don't usually insult my guests before they appear in front of the camera but if I describe this, er, character as a bloodsucker, I'm sure you will all understand for it is none other than that famous star of horror films, Vlad the Drac.'

The audience applauded warmly and Vlad was carried on lying on a red velvet cushion with gold tassels. Barry Slogan put the cushion on his lap.

'Well, Vlad' he commented. 'So you're getting the red cushion treatment.'

'That's right, Bas,' replied Vlad. 'I'm too weak to fly 'cos I'm recovering from a horrendous traumatic experience.'

'Yes, I believe you spent part of the night alone in the Chamber of Horrors.'

A murmur of sympathy ran through the audience.

'That's right,' replied Vlad.

'Would you like to tell us about it?' suggested Barry Slogan.

'No,' replied Vlad. 'Never. Don't ask me to relive those hours, they were too horrible to describe. All those people and not a single vampire. Not even Great Uncle Ghitza. No, I don't want to talk about it,' and Vlad fell back on his cushion, his hand on his forehead.

'Oh,' said Barry Slogan, a bit surprised.

'Vlad did it,' yelled Dad. 'I knew he would. Poor old Slogan doesn't know what to say. Vlad nonplussed him.'

'Well, perhaps you'd like to talk about your new film with Malcolm Meilberg, "Marauding Monsters of the Outer Galaxy"?'

Vlad brightened up. 'Oh yes, I'll talk about that.' And for five minutes Vlad talked about the film and how it was all about a brave and good vampire and that there were some monsters and people in it but they weren't very important and that everyone should go and see it or get vampirised.

'Well, thank you very much, Vlad.' said Barry Slogan. 'Now, before you go, tell me, and I'm sure the viewers at home want to know too, do you ever frighten anyone? I mean, everyone knows you're a vegetarian but does *anyone* ever take you seriously?'

'Well, it's strange that you should ask me that tonight,' replied Vlad, 'because a funny thing happened to me on my way to the studio. The chauffeur you sent to pick me up wouldn't let me into his car 'cos he was so scared that I'd vampirise him.'

Barry Slogan laughed. 'And why was that, Vlad?' he asked.

''Cos I said to him, "Let the light vanish – the eye of the vampire cannot suffer the light to shine in his eyes. Ah, the light begins to fade, the appetite of the vampire can no longer be suppressed. Blood, blood, I need blood! Let every human beware, the vampire, the beast of the night is abroad, seeking the only food that can satisfy his hunger - *blood!*"'

And Vlad got up from his pillow and flew over to Barry Slogan, who shrieked and rushed away. The audience began to shriek too and lay down under their seats.

'Catch that vampire,' yelled someone.

'Can't catch me,' shouted Vlad, flying up to the roof and shaking the lights. 'The blood of the vampire is roused. Let people beware.'

'What should we do?' asked a worried cameraman.

'Get the woman who came with him,' called another.' Quickly.'

So Gran was called and rushed into the television studio.

'Great Uncle Ghitza,' called Vlad, 'I hope you are

looking down and seeing me, your great nephew Vlad, exacting a terrible revenge on people for your untimely end. The eyes of the public are upon me as I exact vengeance for your murder by telephone.'

Gran stood in the middle of the stage and said in a very stern tone,

'Vlad, come here this minute. What disgraceful behaviour! Now, you come here and get into my handbag without another word.'

'Shan't,' said Vlad. 'You must quail to see the vampire at night, lusting for his meal of blood, flying with steely gaze towards his prey.'

Gran was not at all put out.

'Vlad, I've had enough of this nonsense. If I have to ask you to come down here just one more time it's no washing-up liquid for two days.'

'You wouldn't do that,' exclaimed Vlad in horror.

'Oh, wouldn't I?' countered Gran. 'You needn't be in two minds about that. Now, if you're not in my handbag by the count of five, that's what will happen. One, two, three . . .'

Vlad flew over to Gran and climbed into her handbag muttering, 'Spoilsport. Just when I was having a bit of fun! People always spoil everything. Poor Old Vlad, Poor Little Drac.'

Gran snapped her handbag shut and everyone got off the floor and cheered her. Gran smiled and waved and backed away as fast as she could.

'Well, thank you, Vlad the Drac,' said Barry Slogan, straightening his tie and smoothing his hair. 'And never let anyone say this programme is predictable. Now, I hope you will pardon my French when I say I'm sure you all agree that this has been a bloody good show. Now, for our next guest . . .'

Dad switched the television off.

'Ha,' he said. 'Now everyone who watched that programme will know what I've had to put up with over the years.'

'He was really awful,' commented Paul. 'Even you must admit that, Judy.'

'He just got a bit over-excited,' replied Judy. 'He was only playing and I bet everyone enjoyed it really.'

When Gran and Vlad got back, Dad made her a cup of tea.

'Thanks, dear,' she said. 'I really need that.'

'Never thought you'd be a TV star,' Dad told her.

'Me neither,' agreed Gran. 'But unexpected things happen around that vampire.'

'I thought you were great, Gran,' Paul told her.

'Fast thinking, Gran,' said Judy admiringly.

'Well, I'm glad you all thought I was all right,' smiled Gran. 'There was no time to be scared of all those people,' and she opened her handbag to get a tissue. Vlad stuck his head out.

'Were you lot watching me?' he asked. 'Wasn't I great? I scared all those people. I said, "As the light fades from the sky, the vampire looms in the darkness, no human is safe as with fiery eye he surveys the world . . ."'

Dad jumped up and grabbed Vlad, pushing him back into Gran's bag and shut it firmly.

'Hope you don't mind, mother,' he said, 'but I think we've all had enough of the blood of the vampire for one night.'

And no one disagreed.

6

Count Vladski the Dracski

'Letter for you, Vlad,' said Paul, picking up the post from the mat.

'Is it from Romania?' asked Vlad.

'No,' said Paul, looking at the stamp. 'It's from England.'

'What can it be?' mused the vampire. 'You open it.'

So Paul opened the envelope and read, 'Malcolm Meilberg requests the pleasure of the company of Vlad the Drac at the Royal Command Performance showing of his new film "Marauding Monsters of the Outer Galaxy" next Friday at the Pantheon Cinema, Leicester Square.'

'An invitation,' squeaked Vlad. 'Oh, I do like invitations. But what does it mean?'

'It means,' replied Paul, 'that you are invited to the first night of your film.'

'Yes, I know that,' said Vlad impatiently. 'But what is a Royal Command Performance?'

'That means that members of the Royal Family will be there.'

'Ah,' said Vlad, looking very excited. 'And will I meet them, then?'

'I suppose so,' answered Paul.

'Gosh,' said Vlad. 'Me meeting royalty! I wonder what Great Uncle Ghitza would make of that.'

'From what you tell me about your Great Uncle Ghitza, he'd just want to vampirise them.'

'Well,' replied Vlad, 'I wouldn't be too sure about that. Even Great Uncle Ghitza drew the line at royalty. After all, we're descended from royalty ourselves.'

'Oh, come off it, Vlad,' said Paul. 'You're making it up.'

'I am not,' said the vampire indignantly. 'The fact is, I'm of noble stock, I have blue blood in my veins and, if I'm to meet with Kings and Queens and so on, it is only fitting that I should have a title to reflect my descent from an ancient line of kings.'

'What kind of a title?' asked Paul.

'How about King Vlad the Great of Transylvania?' suggested Vlad.

'But you're not the King,' Paul pointed out. 'They could easily check up.'

'I suppose so,' groaned Vlad. 'Poor Old Vlad, Poor

Little Drac. Have to think of something else.'

'How about Sir Vlad the Drac?' offered Paul.

'You are so unimaginative,' complained the vampire. 'That won't do at all. I want a name that sounds romantic and Romanian. I think I shall be the Grand Duke Vladimir Dracorovitch Alexander Romanov Slobovitch Bumphimovski, known as Olya to his friends, Grand Master of the Order of the Castle, Fellow of the Knights of the Blood of St Ghitza and Companion of the Vampires of the Cold Bath. Now, what do you think of that?'

Paul groaned. 'It's very long-winded, Vlad. Every-one would go to sleep before you got to the end.'

'Can't have that,' said Vlad quickly. 'Oh dear, I don't know — yes I do, yes I do, I've got it. I'm a genius, a genius. How about Count Vladski the Dracski?'

'Sounds a bit funny to me,' said Paul.

'Funny!' exclaimed Vlad. 'Funny! you don't know what you're talking about. It's brilliant, absolutely brilliant, pure genius, that's what it is.'

So when Vlad next visited Mum at the hospital he told her all about being Count Vladski the Dracski.

'Fancy that,' he told Mum. 'I spent so much time under that stone that I completely forgot my real title.'

82

The Stones all looked a bit doubtful about Vlad's new title but didn't say anything. Vlad flew over to the cot.

'Hello, snoglet,' he said. 'Look at what your Uncle Vladski the Dracski has got here, an invitation to meet royalty.'

'Goo,' said the baby.

'She's very impressed,' he told the Stones. 'She's lovely, isn't she? Oh, I do like babies; well done, Mum. She's absolutely smashing.'

'Thanks, Vlad,' said Mum. 'Now, tell me all about this Royal Command Performance.'

So Vlad told Mum all that he knew.

'There will be all these famous people there — and just one famous vampire, me — and we'll all watch the film and then we will all get introduced to the Royals.'

'Sounds good,' said Mum.

'Sounds a bit frightening to me.' admitted Vlad. 'Now that I think about it, could I take Judy and then I could sit on her shoulder? I'll need a friendly shoulder to sit on and Mal will be very busy.'

'Would you like that, Judy?' asked Mum.

Judy looked up from admiring her new sister.

'Ooo, yes, Mum,' she replied.

'What about me?' demanded Paul indignantly.

'Well, what about you?' replied Vlad. 'I only need one shoulder to sit on.'

'I don't think Judy should go if Paul can't go too,' pronounced Dad.

Vlad sighed deeply. 'Oh, all right, I'll ring Mal and tell him they are both coming, if you insist.'

'What is all this Count Vladski the Dracski stuff?' asked Dad while Vlad was out of the room. 'It sounds pretty phoney to me."

It's better than the other name he thought of,' Paul told his father. 'He wanted to be the Grand Duke something something something Bumphimovski.'

'Ha,' said Dad. 'I wish someone would go and bump Vlad offski.'

'Now, don't be unkind,' said Mum. 'If it's important for Vlad to think he's descended from royalty, don't spoil it for him.'

So the next evening Paul and Judy sat waiting for the taxi to come to take them to the cinema. Vlad had spent most of the day getting ready and looked elegant in his best suit. Gran ironed a shirt for him.

'I'm glad you're here,' he told her. 'I like having you around.'

'That's nice,' Gran replied. 'But I'm going home

tonight, they don't seem to need me round here any more.'

'I need you,' said Vlad, getting tearful.

'But so does Allan.'

'Who's Allan?' asked Vlad.

'My husband,' she told him.

'The Lord High's pater,' shrieked Vlad. 'I'll vampirise him.'

'No, you won't,' said Gran. 'But I hope you'll come and visit us sometime.'

The children and Vlad waved Gran goodbye as she drove off.

'She's a very nice lady,' commented Vlad. 'I shall miss her,' and he stood in front of the mirror holding his gloves and admiring himself.

'I look very handsome,' he told Judy. 'Even if I do say it myself. Count Vladski the Dracski is a very good-looking vampire.'

'Umm,' said Judy. 'But I think you need a few medals or something. Counts usually have things like that.'

'You're right!' cried Vlad, burying his head in his hands. 'You're right, I need some medals and I don't have any. We'll have to cancel everything. Ring up Mal and tell him I can't come.'

'Hang on,' said Judy calmly. 'Don't panic.'

'Don't panic, she says!' exclaimed the vampire. 'We've got a crisis on our hands and she says don't panic!'

'Look' said Judy. 'I've got all these chocolates covered in gold paper to look like coins. I'll stick one on a piece of ribbon from my doll and you can wear it round you.'

'Good thinking,' said Vlad. 'As people go, Judith, you are not at all bad, and that is high praise from a vampire.'

'Thanks, Vlad,' said Judy. 'And look, there's our taxi. We'd better go.'

Vlad suddenly jumped in the air. 'Oh, I nearly forgot I've got to visit the cellar,' and he leapt up, flew into the kitchen and then disappeared into the darkness of the cellar.

'What does he do down there every day?' puzzled Paul.

'I don't know,' replied Judy. 'But if you ask him about it he bites your head off.'

Outside, the cab hooted for them.

'Come on, Vlad,' yelled the children. 'The cab's here.'

Vlad flew up from the cellar, slammed the door and, sitting on Judy's shoulder, proclaimed, 'Lead on. Count Vladski the Dracski, Companion of the

Order of the Cold Bath, and his entourage are ready to depart.'

Much to everyone's surprise and relief, Vlad behaved beautifully at the Royal Command Performance and was a big hit. Vlad fell asleep in the taxi on the way home and Judy popped him into his drawer without waking him.

The next morning Vlad came downstairs sitting triumphantly on Judy's shoulder. Dad was already there, sitting quietly at the kitchen table eating his breakfast and reading the paper. Judy put Vlad on the table, while she went to find some cornflakes for herself and some washing-up liquid for Vlad.

'Morning, squire,' said Vlad cheerfully.

'Morning,' said Dad absent-mindedly, concentrating on the newspaper article he was reading. Vlad lay on his back so that he could read what was on the other side of Dad's paper.

'It's me,' he yelled. 'Look, there's a picture of me and the princess.'

'Do you mind?' snapped Dad, looking over the paper. 'I'm trying to read and drink a cup of tea.'

'But there's a picture of *me*,' squeaked the vampire.

Dad gave a deep sigh and turned the paper round.

'Look,' said Vlad proudly. 'There.'

And there was a picture with a headline underneath, 'Princess declares Drac to be perfectly sweet.'

'Huh,' said Dad dismissively. 'Perfectly sweet, indeed. She should only know.'

'You're just jealous,' replied Vlad. 'I bet no princess ever described you as "perfectly sweet", nor is ever likely to.'

Judy came to the table with her cereal and Vlad's drink.

'Look,' he yelled. 'Look, it's my picture in the paper and the princess thinks I'm perfectly sweet.'

'That's lovely, Vlad,' said Judy, looking nervously at her father who was already buried in his newspaper again.

'Lovely,' shrieked Vlad. 'It's more than that, it's absolutely super, splendiferous and ultra-plus wonderful,' and he began to sing loudly:

'I'm the Tops,
I'm the Coliseum,
I'm the Tops,
I'm the Louvre Museum,
I'm a melody from a symphony by Strauss,
I'm an Easter Bonnet,
A Shakespeare Sonnet,
I'm Mickey Mouse!'

Dad glared at him, but Vlad went on:

> *'I'm the Tops,*
> *I'm the Tower of Pisa,*
> *I'm the smile on the Mona Lisa.'*

'Be quiet!' snapped Dad.
Still Vlad took no notice.

> *'I'm the Tops, I'm Inferno's Dante,*
> *I'm the nose on the Great Durante.'*

'I'm trying to read the paper,' yelled Dad.
'What's stopping you?' said Vlad, and dancing round the table he continued:

> *'I'm the Tops,*
> *I'm Mahatma Gandhi,*
> *I'm the Tops*
> *I'm Napoleon brandy,*
> *I'm the purple light of a summer night in Spain,*
> *I'm the National Gallery,*
> *I'm Rod Stewart's salary,*
> *I'm cellophane.'*

'If you don't stop that racket,' said Dad, 'I'll do something nasty.'

'You're a worthless cheque, you're a total wreck, a flop,
'Cos baby if you're the bottom, I'm the top!'

sang Vlad and with his arms outstretched he backed
away from Dad and fell straight into Dad's cup of
tea.

'For goodness sake!' yelled Dad. 'I'm trying to have
a quiet breakfast, Suzanne and the baby are coming
home today and I want a bit of p and q.'

'Well then, don't put your tea-cup where I'll fall
into it,' complained Vlad. 'I sometimes think that's
why cups of tea were invented, so that I could fall
into them.'

'Why don't you look where you're going then?'
snapped Dad.

'I couldn't,' replied the vampire, climbing out of
the cup. 'I was walking backwards.'

'Well then, don't walk backwards,' yelled an infuriated Dad.

'Look at me,' moaned Vlad. 'I'm all wet and I smell
of tea,' and he shook himself like a dog, spraying
Dad and Judy. Dad flung down his newspaper.

'I can't stand it,' he shouted. 'Not for another
moment. Judy, find me that fly swat.'

'Oh Dad,' said Judy. 'Vlad didn't mean to annoy

you, he just got a bit excited.'

'I don't believe it,' growled Dad. 'He loves annoy-ing me. That's all he lives for, and I'm going to swat him.'

'You promised you wouldn't,' Vlad reminded him.

'Well, I'm about to break my promise,' announced Dad.

Vlad decided that Dad meant what he said and that discretion was the better part of valour and flew up to a shelf and hid behind a plant.

'Aha,' shrieked Dad. 'I won't need to swat him. I'll have lots of fun using him as an Aunt Sally.'

'No, Dad,' pleaded Judy. 'Please leave Vlad alone.'

'No way,' said Dad, his eyes gleaming and he picked up some tomatoes from the vegetable rack and started to throw them at Vlad. Vlad kept ducking out of the way, hiding behind plants and dishes.

'Stop it, Dad,' said Judy urgently. 'You'll break something.'

'I don't care,' said Dad. 'I'm having such a good time. Ha, no more tomatoes. Right, I'll start on the eggs. Do you want an egg to throw, Judy?'

Seeing that Dad was serious, Vlad pushed open the lid of a teapot and jumped in yelling, 'I surrender.'

'Dad, Vlad's trying to surrender,' Judy told her father.

Vlad lifted the teapot lid and waved a white handkerchief. But Dad was having too much fun and ignored the white flag and an egg landed right on

Vlad, who disappeared back into the teapot. Just as Judy was wondering what would happen when her father ran out of eggs, Mum walked into the kitchen carrying the baby.

'Nick, what on earth are you doing?' she cried.

Dad stopped and looked at her.

'Oh, hello, love, I wasn't expecting you. I was going to come and fetch you later.'

'I took a taxi,' said Mum. 'And it seems just as well that I did.'

'Well, yes, dear,' said Dad beginning to look sheepish. 'I'm afraid Vlad and I were having a little quarrel.'

'Well, I think it's too bad of you,' said Mum tearfully. 'I've only been away a few days.'

Vlad came out of the teapot and flew over to Mum.

'Welcome home,' he said. 'It's lovely to see you and the snoglet.'

'You look terrible,' said Mum, wrinkling her nose. 'And you smell horrid, too.'

'Sorry,' said Vlad. 'It's the mixture of tea, eggs and mouldy tomatoes.'

'I just don't understand what's going on,' said Mum, sitting down.

'It was all my fault,' said Vlad quickly. 'I annoyed

94

Dad so much that he's been throwing things at me. But you're not to be cross with him, as it really was my fault.'

'That's all well and good,' protested Mum, 'but just look at all the mess.'

'Don't give it a thought,' said Vlad. 'You go upstairs and have a nice rest. I'll clear up and Judy will make you a nice cup of tea.'

Mum went upstairs helped by Dad. As Dad left the kitchen he caught Vlad's eye.

'Thanks,' he said. 'And sorry.'

'You can thank your lucky stars,' said Vlad, 'that I am a vampire with a noble and forgiving nature. Come, Judith, lots of warm, soapy water, please, and let's go. Poor Old Vladski, Poor Little Dracski.'

7

The Day Out

'That was nice of you to help Dad out like that,' Judy commented to Vlad, as he finished cleaning up the kitchen.

'Jolly well was,' agreed Vlad. 'Particularly after he'd behaved so badly to me.'

'Why did you do it?' asked Judy;

'I'll let you into a secret,' said Vlad, 'if you promise you won't tell anyone, never, ever, ever, ever, no matter what happens.'

'All right,' agreed Judy.

'Well, I like Dad really,' confessed Vlad. 'Not liking him is just a game, but don't you dare ever tell anyone or I'll vampirise you.'

'Your secret is safe with me,' Judy assured him. 'Come on, let's pop you into the washing machine to clean you up.'

So Judy put Vlad in the washing machine with a little detergent on a mild wash. As he went round in the machine, he waved to Judy. After being spun and tumbled, Vlad was clean and dry.

'I smell delicious,' he said. 'Come on, let's go and see Zoë.'

They found Mum and Zoë sitting in the front room with Dad and Paul.

'Can I hold her?' asked Judy.

'Of course,' said Mum. 'Just remember to support her head.'

Judy took Zoë and Vlad told Mum about his meeting with the princess and how much she liked him.

'I've already heard about this twice,' complained Dad.

Mum glanced at him and decided that it would be a good idea to separate Dad and Vlad.

'Why don't you two take Vlad out for the day?' she said brightly to Judy and Paul.

'Oh Mum,' said Paul. 'Last time we did that it was awful. Vlad hijacked a bus, scared everyone in the Bloody Tower and finally got locked in the Chamber of Horrors.'

'Wasn't my fault,' moaned the vampire.

'Mum, you promised us we could stay home and play with Zoë when you came back from the hospital and now you want us to go out with Vlad again,' complained Judy.

'Poor Old Judy, Poor Little Paul,' commented Vlad. Mum ignored him.

'Yes, I know, darlings, but if you would do it just this once, it would be a great help to me.'

'There's no point,' exploded Dad. 'If he stays here he's in trouble with me and if he goes out he's in trouble with everybody else.'

'I can't win,' complained Vlad. 'Poor Old Vlad, Poor Little Drac.'

'Come on, Vlad,' said Mum. 'Be nice, go out with the children and you can choose what to have for supper.'

'You're trying to bribe me,' said Vlad. 'And you have succeeded. I fancy a nice tin of rust remover.'

'You'll get it,' promised Mum.

'See that I do,' replied Vlad. 'Vampires take a very dim view of broken promises.'

So Judy and Paul found themselves out with Vlad yet again waiting for a bus.

'Well,' said the vampire. 'Where are we going?'

'Don't know,' said Judy.

'You choose,' said Paul

'Well,' stated Vlad, 'you used to say that I'd end up in a museum or a zoo.'

'Yes?' said the children questioningly.

'Well, take me to a museum and then to the zoo. After Dad's deplorable behaviour I just might prefer one of them.'

'Which museum do you think Vlad would have been put in?' Judy asked Paul.

'The Natural History, I suppose,' replied Paul. 'You know, the one with the animals and dinosaurs.'

'Dinosaurs?' squeaked Vlad. 'Like I had in my space-ship in "Marauding Monsters of the Outer Galaxy"?'

'That's right,' said Paul.

'Well, then,' said Vlad. 'Let's go. What are we waiting for?'

'A bus,' Paul told him.

A bus came along quickly. Paul and Judy began to clamber up the steps when the driver saw them.

'Off,' he said brusquely. 'Hop it. I'm not having that vampire on my bus again. Last time he had me driving all over London.'

'Oh, please,' said Judy. 'He won't do it again.'

'Off,' snapped the bus driver. 'Hurry up, you're holding up the bus.'

Reluctantly Paul and Judy climbed down. Vlad yelled from Paul's shoulder, 'I didn't want to go in your rotten old bus, anyway.'

'All right, Vlad,' said Paul, 'it's pocket time. Come

on, into my anorak pocket.'

'It's not fair,' moaned Vlad. 'I wasn't even going to hijack that bus.'

'Well, you've obviously got a reputation with bus drivers,' Judy explained to him. 'You're a notorious, infamous vampire and they don't want you on their buses.'

'Ha,' said Vlad beaming. 'They're all scared of being vampirised. When the sun sets in the west, the blood of the vampire is afire . . .'

'Not another word about the blood of the vampire,' snapped Paul. 'Now, come on, there's another bus coming. Quick, into my pocket.'

So, muttering to himself, Vlad flew into Paul's pocket. Soon they arrived at the Natural History Museum. As the children hopped off the bus, Vlad stuck his head out of Paul's pocket and yelled at the driver, 'I fooled you, I fooled you.'

Paul pushed him down and they ran off towards the museum, only letting Vlad emerge as they neared the entrance.

They walked in through the glass doors and stood in the huge central hall of the museum. Vlad looked out of Paul's pocket.

'Gosh,' he said as he looked at the vaulted roof and

the Gothic arches, 'it's very big, isn't it?'

In the middle of the main hall was the skeleton of a diplodocus. From the tip of its tail to its nose it was twenty-six metres long, with a long, long neck and a tiny head. Vlad looked at it hard.

'What is it?' he asked.

'It's a dinosaur,' Judy told him.

'It doesn't look much like the one in the film,' commented Vlad.

'That's just its skeleton,' explained Paul. 'The bones under the skin.'

'Why only his bones?' asked Vlad. 'Why not a proper dinosaur?'

'Because they're extinct,' continued Paul. 'They're a dead species.'

'Like vampires nearly are,' said Vlad gloomily.

'Not while you're around,' said Judy encouragingly. 'You've had five children. You're doing well.'

'I know,' agreed Vlad. 'But Mrs Vlad won't have any more. Do you think they've got a skeleton of a vampire here?'

'I don't think so,' said Judy.

'So if I'd been sent here, would they have turned me into a skeleton?'

'Not until you were dead,' Judy assured him.

'It's a bit creepy,' said Vlad and he flew up and sat on the dinosaur's head.

'It's got a very small head,' he shouted down at Judy and Paul.

A keeper came running up.

'Come down,' he yelled at Vlad. 'No one is allowed to touch the dinosaur; it's very delicate.'

A small crowd began to gather round the dinosaur. A child in a school party recognized Vlad.

'It's Vlad the Drac,' he said loudly. 'I saw him on television.'

'Hello, Vlad,' the rest of the class called up.

'Hello, kiddiwinks,' Vlad called back, and he sat down on the dinosaur's neck.

'I'm going to get the director,' declared the keeper. 'I don't know what to do. There's nothing in the rules about vampires.'

More and more people came into the main hall of the museum. Vlad, seeing his audience get bigger, ran up and down the dinosaur's backbone and flew in and out of its ribs. The crowd got bigger and bigger. Nothing Judy or Paul said made any impact on Vlad.

'It's hopeless, Judy,' groaned Paul. 'Now that he's got an audience, he'll stay up there all day.'

A minute or two later the Director came running into the hall with the keeper.

'Does this — er — creature belong to anyone?' he asked.

'Here we go,' muttered Paul, and he and Judy went up to the Director.

'He's ours, that is, he's staying with us."

Can't you persuade him to come down?' asked the director, looking very worried.

'We've tried,' explained Judy. 'It's all the people looking at him that are the problem. He likes to show off. If you could get everyone to leave, I expect he'd get bored and come down.'

'Right,' said the Director, and he told the group of keepers who had gathered to empty the hall.

'Everyone out, please,' they said. 'Please leave the hall quietly. The dinosaur is in danger of collapsing, it's not safe.'

Reluctantly people filed out of the hall. The school-children craned their necks to look behind them.

'Bye, Vlad,' they called.

'Come back!' shouted Vlad. 'Don't go! Come back here this instant. I'm going to do a song and dance. Look! Look at me!

'I'm off to see the wizard,
The wonderful Wizard of Oz.'

he sang at the top of his voice and he danced up and down the dinosaur's spine.

'Don't,' shouted the Director. 'The dinosaur will collapse, it's very delicate . . .'

But it was too late. The skeleton shook, wavered for a minute and then it crashed to the ground. Vlad shrieked and then was buried under the crashing bones. Judy and Paul and the Director and the keepers began to search for Vlad under the bones.

'Poor old Vlad,' said Judy. 'I hope he's all right.'

'Here he is,' called the Director, as he lifted a pile of bones. Vlad sat up looking a bit surprised and rubbed his head.

'Well,' he informed the group standing round him, 'I certainly don't want to live in this museum.'

'Over my dead body,' said the Director sternly. 'Now, come on up to my study, you've got some explaining to do.'

'Poor Old Vlad, Poor Little Drac,' moaned the vampire as Judy lifted him up carefully and carried him to the Director's office.

They all sat down and the Director sat behind his desk and looked very serious.

'Do you realize,' he said to Vlad, 'that you have just destroyed one of the best dinosaur skeletons in the world?'

'I'm sorry,' said Vlad, looking very upset. 'I didn't mean to. I just got excited, you see.'

'It will cost a lot of money to put that skeleton together again. Fortunately, no bones were broken, but it will take time and money to reconstruct it.'

'We haven't got any money,' said Judy, 'and neither has Vlad. But if I could make a phone call, we know someone who has.'

So Judy phoned Malcolm Meilberg, who groaned and said he'd come straight to the museum.

When he arrived Malcolm Meilberg was taken to see Vlad's handiwork.

'What a mess,' exclaimed the film producer. 'He's made even more of a mess of your dinosaur than he did of mine.'

'You mean he makes a habit of this kind of thing?' asked the Director in horror. 'He's a menace.'

'I couldn't agree more,' said Malcolm Meilberg. 'But I'm willing to help. I'll make a film of you rebuilding the dinosaur. It will interest children and I'm willing to pay all the costs of reconstructing the dinosaur.'

'A film!' said Vlad, brightening up. 'Can I be in it.'

'No,' said everyone emphatically.

'All right, all right,' sulked Vlad. 'Don't all shout at once.'

'Now, you two,' said the Director, 'I want you to take Vlad away at once and if he ever comes in here again I'll have him arrested on the spot.'

'I definitely do *not* intend to live in a museum,' announced Vlad at the top of his voice as they left the building. 'Not a nice place at all.'

Judy and Paul sat on a bench outside the museum.

'I suppose we'd better go home,' said Judy. 'I'm exhausted.'

'Me, too,' agreed Paul. 'In the circumstances, I don't think Mum would mind.'

'Home?' interrupted Vlad. 'Home? Don't be ridiculous. It's only the morning and I haven't been to the zoo yet. If you take me home, I'll quarrel with Dad straight away.'

'If we take you to the zoo, do you promise to behave?' asked Judy. 'No more song and dance acts?'

'I promise,' agreed Vlad. 'I'm really sorry about the

skeleton. It was very bad of me, but I just got over-excited.'

'If Mal hadn't bailed you out, you'd have been in dead trouble,' Paul pointed out. 'And us with you.'

'I know, I know,' said the vampire. 'I feel very bad about it all. If you take me to the zoo, I'll be very good.'

'Come on, then,' said Judy. 'The zoo it is.'

'We may regret this,' groaned Paul.

'Don't worry,' said Judy. 'The animals at the zoo aren't delicate. I think Vlad may get the worst of it there.'

They caught a bus to the zoo. Vlad snuggled inside Judy's anorak as they paid to go in.

'It looks better than the museum,' Vlad commented, looking out over Judy's anorak. Then he heard a lion roar and ducked quickly.

'It's all right, Vlad,' Judy told him, 'they're all in cages.'

Vlad peeped out. 'They're very big and fierce,' he said. 'I'm scared.'

'What a relief,' said Paul. 'Vlad's too scared to muck around.'

So the children bought ice-creams and ate them while watching the kangaroos.

'Amazing the way they move, isn't it?' commented Judy.

'Yeah,' agreed Paul. 'They use their tails to propel themselves along.'

'What do you think, Vlad?' asked Judy, looking down. 'Oh Paul, Vlad's gone. Where can he be?'

'There,' said Paul, pointing to a kangaroo. Judy looked and there was Vlad waving from the kangaroo's pouch.

'Better than a bus any day,' he shouted.

After a while, Vlad got bored. He thanked the kangaroo politely and flew back to Judy.

'She was nice,' he said. 'but I don't think I'd like the zoo, I'd be caged in. Couldn't do what I liked.'

'Where would you like to go next?' Judy asked him.

'I want to see the bats,' Vlad informed her. 'Maybe there are some vampire bats.'

So they went into the reptile house.

'It's a bit smelly,' complained Vlad, wrinkling up his nose.

Eventually they found the bats who were hanging upside down. Vlad tried to talk to them by hanging upside down too on the outside of the cage but he got no response.

'Very anti-social, these bats,' he said. 'They didn't

want to talk to me at all. No, the zoo's not for me. I've decided to stay with you and Mum and the Lord High and the snoglet.'

'I was afraid that that was what you would decide,' said Paul gloomily. 'So can we go home now?'

'We can,' agreed the vampire.

They walked to the gate via the elephant house. Vlad looked up at the elephants admiringly.

'They're very big, aren't they?' he commented. 'But, look, he doesn't seem to mind the little bird sitting on his head. I think I'll try it,' and he flew up and sat on the elephant's head. Vlad was just beginning to show off for the people with cameras in the crowd, when the elephant decided to wash herself. She filled her trunk with water.

'That elephant is going to squirt Vlad,' said Judy giggling. 'Do you think we should warn him, Paul?'

'Definitely not,' laughed Paul. 'Let him have it. Here she goes,' and the elephant raised her trunk and whoosh, Vlad was drenched in cold water. He shrieked as he fell, soaking, off the elephant's head. All around him cameras clicked.

'Stop it,' yelled Vlad at the photographers, and flew over to Judy and tried to climb into her anorak.

'Go away,' she yelled. 'You're soaking wet.'

'I'm freezing,' whimpered the vampire. 'I'll catch my death of cold.'

'Serve you right,' said Paul, grinning.

'Do something,' said Vlad. 'I can't stand here in these wet clothes.'

So Paul and Judy bought some souvenirs in the zoo shop and asked for a plastic bag to put them in. Vlad climbed into the bag and took off his wet clothes and, wrapped in Paul's scarf, he sat in the bag and sulked while they carried him home.

When they got in Mum said, smiling,

'So did you all have a nice day?'

Judy and Paul were silent.

'I have had a very trying day,' Vlad told her. 'However, you will be relieved to hear that I have decided not to go and live in a museum or the zoo but will continue to be in residence here. Now I shall retire for the night to the cellar. Will you please have my breakfast ready and on the table by eight-thirty. I wish you all a very good night.'

8
Fireworks

After the events at the zoo and the museum, Judy and Paul were reluctant to take Vlad out.

'I can't understand it,' moaned Vlad. 'You are being most unreasonable. After all, anyone can make a mistake – even people. Poor Old Vlad, Poor Little Drac.'

The children went back to school and Mum and Dad were too involved with the new baby to take much notice of Vlad. The vampire began to feel bored.

'I've got nothing to do,' he complained to Dad. 'You don't need my help and I'm bored.'

'I know,' agreed Dad. 'So why don't you go home? You've seen Zoë, you've congratulated Mum, you've been to your first night, you've been on television, you've wrecked a dinosaur, you've been in the papers regularly, you've driven me round the bend, so what do you have to stay for? Seriously, don't you think it's time you went home?'

'No,' replied Vlad.

'Why not?' enquired an infuriated Dad.

'Unfinished business,' Vlad told him.

'What kind of business?' snapped Dad.

'Vampire business,' replied Vlad. 'And now, if you don't mind, I shall take a piece of meat and go and play in the cellar.'

'I just don't understand what a vegetarian like you does with all this meat,' said Dad.

'Meat, meat, glorious meat,
Nothing quite like it for warming your feet,'

sang Vlad and he disappeared into the cellar.

'Vlad doesn't want to go home,' Dad told Mum. 'Some nonsense about unfinished business.'

'Well, we'll have to talk to him,' said Mum firmly. 'And tell him that he's got to go. Look, here are a stack of letters from his wife. She's obviously missing him and he doesn't even bother to open the letters.'

'I know,' said Dad, brightening up. 'I'll go and buy Vlad a ticket back to Romania, then if he's got a ticket he'll *have* to go.'

When Vlad emerged from the cellar Dad told him about the ticket and Vlad was very annoyed.

'I'll go when *I* want,' he said, 'not when you decide.'

'You don't have to go at all,' replied Dad. 'If you go and stay somewhere other than this house, you can stay as long as you please.'

'I always stay in this house,' grumbled Vlad. 'I like it here and I think you're being rotten,' and he flew out into the garden and slammed the door.

'I told him,' Dad informed Mum. 'He didn't like it.'

'Where is he?' asked Mum.

'Out in the garden sulking,' Dad told her.

'Good,' said Mum. 'I expect he'll cool off a bit out there and we can have a bit of peace and quiet.'

But it was not to be. After a while, there was a long angry ring at the front door.

'I'll go,' said Mum.

The bell rang loudly a second time. Mum opened the door.

'Oh hello, Pete,' she said, seeing the next-door neighbour, Pete Mercer from number 5, standing on the doorstep with two broken pots in his hand.

'Look at my pots,' he said angrily. 'All broken, and more like that in my greenhouse.'

'I'm sorry,' said Mum, 'but what's it got to do with us?'

'It's that vampire of yours,' replied Pete Mercer.

'He locked my dog in the greenhouse. The dog panicked and it's all smashed up.'

'I'm so sorry,' said Mum, horrified. 'We'll pay for all the damage of course.'

'Money's only part of it,' complained Mr Mercer. 'All my seedlings are gone. I've put a lot of love and hard work into my greenhouse. That vampire is a menace.'

'He's going home soon,' said Mum. 'We'll pay for the damage and Nick and the children will come and help you put the greenhouse right.'

Somewhat mollified, Mr Mercer went back home. Mum told Dad what had happened and they both went out into the garden to find Vlad.

'Vlad,' yelled Dad. 'You come here this minute.'

'He's not here,' said Mum.

'He can't have gone far,' insisted Dad. 'He can't fly far. Vlad, where are you?'

They listened hard but there was no reply. Then they heard a cat mewing, loudly and obviously in great distress.

'Look,' said Mum. 'Up there, next door, on the roof. It's Tabby! Poor cat, she's trapped on the roof and she's terrified. We'd better call the fire brigade.'

Dad went off to phone for the fire brigade and while he was gone Mum heard Vlad's voice.

'Ya, boo, you rotten cat. You can stay up there all night and see if I care. You'll get very hungry, hee, hee, hee.'

Mum leaned over the fence of the other neighbour's garden.

'Vlad,' she said in a strict voice. 'What are you doing in the Smiths' garden?'

'Nothing,' said Vlad innocently. 'I'm just sitting in this tree minding my own business.'

'Then why didn't you answer when we called?'

'Didn't hear,' replied the vampire.

'Nonsense,' snapped Mum. 'And what were you saying to the cat?'

'The poor pussy is trapped on the roof,' explained Vlad. 'The branch she climbed along to get on to the roof mysteriously snapped. Look, there it is on the grass. I'm just trying to calm the poor little puss down.'

'You're a liar, Vlad,' said Mum angrily. 'I heard you taunting that poor cat. You broke that branch on purpose. Now come on down.'

'Shan't,' said Vlad. 'Don't want to and you can't make me. You can't get at me up here.'

'Don't you be so sure,' Mum called up. 'The fire brigade is coming to rescue the cat and they'll get you, too.'

'The fire brigade?' said Vlad. 'Oooh, good. I was so bored this afternoon and now lots of exciting things are happening.'

'I wouldn't get too excited about it,' Mum told him, 'because you're in trouble. First of all, you locked the dog at the Mercers' in the greenhouse, and now this. You're in plenty of trouble.'

'Who cares?' yelled Vlad. 'Dad's sending me home

anyway. Might as well be hanged for a sheep as a lamb.'

In the distance they heard the siren of the fire engine.

'Tell them to come and get me,' shouted Vlad. 'I'm ready for them.'

Just as the fire engine stopped outside their house, Paul and Judy arrived home from school. They rushed into the house yelling, 'Mum, Dad, what's happened? Where's the fire? Is everyone all right?'

Seeing that the back door was open, they ran out into the garden. Dad was holding Zoë and both he and Mum were looking up at the tree next door.

'What is it?' gasped Judy.

'What's happened?' demanded Paul.

'Vlad's up in the tree,' Dad explained wearily, 'and the cat's trapped on the roof.'

The firemen came running through the Stones' house with all their ladders and hoses and out into the garden.

'Hope it's all right, sir, if we climb over the fence,' said the chief fireman.

'Yes, of course,' said Dad, watching resignedly as his favourite plants got trampled by the firemen.

'Come and get me,' yelled Vlad from his tree. 'All

right, you flat-footed, bungle-toothed manglewurzels, come and get me! I'm ready for you,' and he shook the tree, so that leaves and twigs fell on the firemen.

'Oh, my gawd,' exclaimed the fireman. 'Who's that?'

'Vlad the Drac,' explained Paul. 'He lives with us when he's in London.'

'*Used* to live with us,' corrected Dad.

'Come on, you lily-livered bunch of no-goods,' shrieked Vlad. 'I'm waiting for you.'

'Bad-mannered, isn't he? Big mouth for such a small — er — thing,' said the fireman. 'I think it's time someone taught him a lesson. Bring the hoses through, lads.'

Soon all the hoses were turned on Vlad and he was drenched.

'Stop it,' he yelled. 'You're soaking me. First the elephant and now you. Poor Old Vlad, Poor Little Drac.'

Soon Vlad and the cat were brought down the ladder. The cat arched its back and hissed at Vlad.

'Help,' yelled Vlad and he ran as fast as he could into the kitchen and slammed the door.

'Serve him right,' said Dad. 'I hope he got a good scare.'

Soon the firemen and the Stones were all sitting

in the kitchen having a cup of tea. Judy put Vlad in the spin dryer to dry him off and get him out of the way. They were all laughing and talking when they heard a banging sound. No one could tell where it was coming from and they started chatting again. Then they heard shouts of 'Help, let me out.'

'It's Vlad,' said Judy. 'He wants to get out of the dryer.'

'Leave him there,' ordered Dad. 'I need a break from Vlad.'

So Vlad was left sulking in the dryer. When Judy eventually let him out, Vlad took himself off to the cellar to lie in Dad's toolbox.

'I don't want to talk to anyone,' he told Judy. 'Under no circumstances do I wish to be disturbed. I have been very badly treated and I'm very cross.'

As soon as Vlad was out of the way, Mum and Dad told Judy and Paul what had happened. They were halfway through the tale when the bell rang.

'I can't stand it,' said Dad. 'You go, Judy, and tell whoever it is that we're not home.'

Judy went to the door and there stood Mrs Smith from number nine, clutching her cat.

'I hear it was your vampire that caused all the trouble,' she told Judy. 'I'm fed up with him. It's one thing after another and this is the last straw.'

'Why, what else has he done?' asked Judy faintly.

'He's been nicking meat out of my fridge,' she replied. 'And he goes flying around at night. It gives me the creeps and I've had enough.'

'Very sorry, Mrs Smith,' said Judy plaintively. 'He's going home soon.'

'I'm glad to hear it,' she snapped. 'And tell your Dad to come round and see me about the damage.'

When Judy went back into the house, Dad said, 'He really must go, Judy. We're quarrelling with everyone; it's never happened before. I'm an easy-going sort of chap, I never argue with anyone except that vampire, and now I'm at it with the neighbours. I can't stand it. I want to enjoy Zoë and I have to spend all my time sorting out the problems Vlad creates.'

'I understand, Dad,' agreed Judy. 'Vlad's gone too far this time. When is his ticket for?'

'Saturday,' said Dad. 'And it can't come fast enough for me.'

The next day Judy asked Vlad why he had quarrelled with the Mercers' dog and the Smiths' cat.

''Cos they're so big,' Vlad told her. 'That rotten dog barks and looks hungry whenever he sees me and the cat ignores me, just licks herself and shows off.

I don't like them and I never will. Don't ask me to make it up with them, 'cos I can't.'

'Then you'll have to stay indoors,' said Judy. 'You can't be trusted to go out.'

All was peaceful until Guy Fawkes night. Judy and Paul gathered wood for the bonfire and counted their fireworks.

'We've got everything except the guy,' said Paul

'What's the guy?' asked Vlad.

'Just a few old clothes stuffed to look like a person,' Paul explained. 'but we haven't any old clothes. They all went off to a jumble sale.'

'I know where there are some old clothes,' said Vlad helpfully. 'If I help you, will you let me come to the bonfire night party?'

'I suppose so,' said Paul.

Soon Vlad returning trailing a bunch of clothes.

'They don't look old,' said Judy. 'Just a bit creased.'

'Oh, they are old,' Vlad assured her. 'Very old.'

So Judy and Paul made a guy and dragged it into the garden.

Mr Mercer stuck his head over the fence.

'What are you children up to?' he yelled. 'You've nicked my gardening clothes from the shed.'

Then Mrs Smith leaned over from her side.

'Have you seen my washing? It's gone off the line.'

'Vlad,' shouted Judy and Paul. But the vampire was nowhere to be seen.

'My hat!' shouted Pete Mercer. 'Look, it's walking on its own.'

And there, sure enough, was the hat running along the path towards the house. Judy ran after the hat and picked it up. Underneath was Vlad, looking a bit surprised.

'Give me my hat back,' he demanded.

Judy picked him up.

'You stole the clothes,' she shouted. 'You said they were old!'

'I thought they were, honest,' said Vlad. 'I was trying to help. Please let me come to the fireworks party.'

The clothes were returned and the preparations for the party went on. Vlad disappeared into the cellar and there were no more problems. Dad agreed that Vlad could come to the fireworks party. Judy and Paul were a bit apprehensive but it all went well. Vlad delighted all the children at the party by sailing up into the sky on rockets, going round and

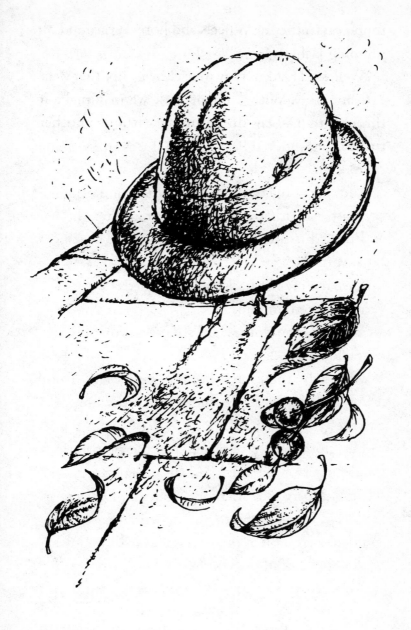

round on Catherine Wheels and hopping around on Jumping Jacks.

'Well,' said Dad, as they were clearing up, 'that went off smoothly. With a bit of luck we may make it through to D-Day on Saturday without another ruckus.'

9

Vlad the Good

After the fireworks party was over, the Stones were so tired they all fell into bed. Judy was just about to fall asleep when she heard a knocking at her window. She looked up and saw Vlad outside.

'Let me in,' he called. 'Its cold out here and it's wet and I want to come in.'

'Leave me alone,' groaned Judy, turning over and going back to sleep. 'I'm so tired.'

After a while, Judy woke up again and, sitting up in bed and rubbing her eyes, wondered what was going on outside. As sleep fell away she realized that Vlad was singing at the top of his voice:

'I'm singin' in the rain,
I'm singin' in the rain,
What a wonderful feelin',
I'm happy again,
I laugh at the clouds,
So high up above,
I'm singin' and dancin' in the rain.'
Dad flung open his bedroom window.

'What on earth do you think you're doing?' he asked.

'I'm singin' and dancin' in the rain,' sang Vlad back at him.

'Well, stop it,' snapped Dad. 'And come in this minute.'

'I have been given to think,' said Vlad, 'that I am not welcome in your house, so if it's all the same to you I'll stay out here.'

'Well, it *isn't* all the same,' yelled Dad. 'You're waking up the whole neighbourhood, as well as keeping us awake.'

'Naughty, naughty,' said Vlad. 'Now who's making a noise?'

Around the area lights began to go on.

'Be quiet out there,' called someone. 'We can't get any sleep.'

'It's that vampire again,' said someone else.

'High time he went home,' said someone else.

Dad was in despair. Mum woke up and the baby began to cry.

'Now look what you've done,' snapped Dad. 'You've annoyed the neighbours *and* you've woken up the baby.'

'Oh, the poor snoglet,' said Vlad. 'I didn't mean to do that. All right, I'll come in, for her sake.'

The next day passed peacefully. Vlad wasn't much to be seen and the Stones assumed that he was down in the cellar.

'Seems to be his favourite place these days,' said Paul.

'At least he can't get into any trouble down there,' said Judy. 'But I do wish I knew what he was doing.'

That evening the Stones heard the sounds of marching and shouting. Judy and Paul looked out of the window.

'They're coming this way,' said Judy. 'And they've got placards.'

'I can hear what they're saying,' cried Paul. 'It's "Vampires out".'

The chanting came nearer. The Stones stood and looked out of the window.

Outside the house a crowd had gathered, carrying banners saying, 'Don't cramp the vamp, send him home,' 'Transfer him to Transylvania,' and 'Send back the Drac.'

They waved the placards in the air and chanted, 'Vlad, Vlad, Vlad, Out, Out, Out.'

Vlad appeared from the cellar.

'Do they want me?' he asked.

'Now look what you've done,' cried Dad. 'All the

neighbours are up in arms.'

'I didn't do anything,' moaned Vlad. 'People are horrid. Poor Old Vlad, Poor Little Drac.'

'Pete Mercer and a couple of the others are coming up to the front door,' said Mum. 'They seem to have a petition or something.'

The front doorbell rang.

'I suppose I'll have to deal with this,' said Dad with a sigh.

'No,' said Vlad calmly. 'I am the problem and I shall deal with it. Judith, please let the people in and I will be happy to receive them.'

So Judy invited Pete Mercer and his delegation into the kitchen. Outside, the chanting continued unabated.

'Now,' said Vlad, standing on the kitchen table drawing himself up to his full height. 'Am I right in understanding that the residents of Willow Road want me to return to Romania?'

'Well, yes,' said Pete Mercer, shuffling around. 'That is the general drift of it. I've got a petition here, signed by everyone in the street, except the Stones, that is.'

'You only had to ask,' said Dad. 'I'd have signed it ten times.'

Vlad ignored him.

'Now, Mr Mercer, perhaps you would like to tell me the reasons for this demonstration.'

'Well,' said Pete Mercer, 'you're terrorizing the animals in this street — my dog, the Smiths' cat. None of the people with animals feel they're safe with you around.'

'I promise, on the sacred memory of Great Uncle Ghitza's telephone, that I won't bother any animals again,' Vlad answered them.

'And,' continued Pete Mercer, 'you woke the whole street up last night, singing "Singin' in the Rain".'

'Sorry about that,' said Vlad, hanging his head. 'I was very bad. I get very excited, you see, wound up, and I don't think about what I'm doing. I promise on Grandmother Natalia's big toe that I won't sing at night again.'

'That's not all,' said Pete Mercer. 'What about stealing the clothes off people's washing lines?'

'I didn't realize they were put out to dry,' Vlad explained. 'I swear by the clasp on Count Dracula's coat never to touch the washing on the line again.'

'There's more,' said Pete Mercer grimly.

'Oh no,' groaned Judy. 'Nothing more.'

'Oh yes there is,' Pete Mercer assured her. 'What about the meat he's been taking out of people's fridges? We've seen him flying around at night and stealing meat. It makes people feel very uneasy having a vampire in their kitchens at night.'

'I *didn't* do that,' complained Vlad. 'That's not fair. I didn't, honestly I didn't.'

'Oh,' said Pete Mercer. 'I see, so there's another vampire flies around this street, is there?'

Vlad suddenly put his hand to his mouth in horror and his eyes grew big as he seemed to take in what Pete Mercer was saying.

'No, no, it was me. Oh dear, I've been losing my memory again. I suffer from that, you know. Do you know, I even forgot that I'm really Count Vladski the Dracski of royal descent? Would you believe that? The Princess was amazed when I told her.'

'I read about you and the Princess in the paper,' said Mrs Smith brightly. 'I told my friend, "That vampire lives in my street," I said.'

'Never mind about the Princess,' said Pete Mercer. 'We're letting him sidetrack us. What about the meat?'

'I took it,' Vlad declaimed. 'It was I, I cannot tell a lie. Guilty as charged. But once again, I give you my word of honour as a vampire, and a Companion of the Grand Order of the Cold Bath, that it will never happen again. From now on your meat and your kitchens are safe. Now can I stay?'

'It's not up to me,' Pete Mercer told him. 'You'll have to convince all the people outside that you've mended your ways.'

'Very well,' said Vlad. 'Let us go out to the front and address the assembled throng.'

So Vlad sat on Pete Mercer's shoulder and together they went out into the street. At the sight of Vlad the group began to chant again.

'Vlad, Vlad, Vlad, Out, Out, Out,' and 'Vampires Out, Vampires Out, Vampires Out.'

Vlad held up his hand for silence.

'Friends, people, men and women, lend me your ears (mine have gone to the laundry and they won't be back for years). No, but seriously, I'm truly sorry for all the trouble I've caused and I have solemnly sworn on my oath as a vampire and a Companion of the Cold Bath never to bother you people again, or even to vampirise you. So I appeal to your British sense of fair play to give me the chance to show you how good a vampire can be. Come on, let's forgive and forget. Let me stay another few days.'

'Promise not to torment the animals,' demanded a woman.

'I promise,' agreed Vlad.

'And what about singing at night?' insisted a man.

'Never again,' promised Vlad.

'Do you agree to stop taking clothes?' asked another.

'I do,' swore Vlad

'And no more meat-stealing and flying around at night?'

'Definitely,' said Vlad firmly. 'No doubt about it. No more meat thefts or night flights.'

'Well, friends,' demanded Pete Mercer. 'Do I have your agreement that Vlad can stay in Willow Road with our consent, provided he sticks to all the promises he just made?'

'Yes,' chorused everyone.

'Thank you, thank you, thank you,' Vlad called. 'You won't regret it.'

'I certainly hope that's true,' breathed Dad. 'Because if it isn't, I shall go crazy.'

'Of course it's true,' said Vlad indignantly. 'I have seen the error of my ways. Now I shall pop down to the cellar for a moment on urgent vampire business, and then I shall clean the house from top to bottom. From now on I shall be a model vampire.'

'Huh,' said Dad. 'I'll believe that when I see it.'

But Vlad was as good as his word. He kept the

house spotlessly clean and was helpful and polite all the time.

After two days of Vlad's excellent behaviour, Judy went to find her mother.

'Mum, can Paul and Vlad and me take Zoë for a walk in the park?'

'Well, I don't know,' said Mum doubtfully.

'You don't have to worry about a thing,' Vlad assured her. 'I will be the grown up in charge.'

'Please, Mum,' begged Paul.

'Well, all right,' said Mum. 'Just for an hour.'

So the three of them went off, with Vlad standing on the pram's handles and giving orders. They walked through the park and looked at the autumn leaves and at the children in the playground. Some of the children recognized Vlad and waved to him. Vlad smiled and waved back. After a while they came to the pond where the model boats sailed. Vlad watched fascinated; he particularly enjoyed the noisy boats, operated by remote control. Suddenly two of the boats collided in the middle of the pond and were stranded in the water. The boys who owned the boats didn't know what to do.

'I can't go home without my boat,' said one, on the

verge of tears. 'My big brother will kill me.'

'Not to worry,' said Vlad. 'You're in luck, son, your fairy vampire is here to help you.' And he flew to the middle of the pond and separated the two boats and then towed them back to their owners. All the people standing round cheered Vlad. The vampire smiled and blew kisses and waved as they left to push the pram to the top of the high hill in the centre of the park. When they got to the top lots of people were flying kites in the wind.

'Are those vampires flapping around up there?' asked Vlad.

'No, they're kites,' Paul assured him.

'Oh,' said Vlad sadly. 'That's a pity.'

But he enjoyed watching the kites weave about in the wind. When one green kite got caught in a tree, its owner began to cry.

'Not to worry,' cried Vlad. 'Super-Drac to the rescue.' And he flew up and freed the stranded kite. Standing on a branch Vlad acknowledged the cheers of the people below.

When the children got home they related Vlad's noble deeds.

'I'm proud of you, Vlad,' said Mum. 'Well done.'

'Think nothing of it,' replied Vlad modestly. 'And

now here is the menu of the local take-away. Will everyone please choose what they would like for supper and I will phone through our order. Pay no attention to the prices. This is on me. Give Dad a night off from the cooking.'

Dad was so amazed by the turn of events that he sat in a silent daze all through the meal.

'Now tonight,' Vlad told Mum and Dad, 'I shall look after the snoglet. I have had a lot of experience with babies. You have a good night's sleep and leave it to your Uncle Vlad to look after everything.'

'I wish I knew what he was up to,' muttered Dad. 'There's more to this than meets the eye.'

'Not at all,' insisted Vlad. 'I have mended my wicked ways. Now, off to bed. I shall keep watch all night.'

Mum and Dad felt a bit insecure about leaving Vlad in charge, but were so tired they went straight off to sleep. Dad was sleeping soundly when he felt a bite on his ear. Vlad was shouting, 'Wake up this minute or I'll bite you properly.'

Dad sat up and glowered at Vlad.

'It's four in the morning. What's the matter with you? Up to your old tricks again?'

'No,' shouted Vlad. 'There's a fire. Look!'

'If this is your idea of a joke —' snapped Dad.

'No,' insisted Vlad, 'there really is a fire! It's over the road. I've called the fire brigade, but I think someone is trapped upstairs.'

Dad jumped out of bed and looked out of the window.

'You're right,' he said, grabbing his dressing gown and slippers. 'Come on.'

They raced downstairs.

'Get a rope,' Vlad shouted. 'I'll go over to the house opposite and tell them the fire brigade is coming.'

So Vlad flew up to the window of the blazing house.

'The fire brigade is on its way,' he called, 'and I'm going to bring you a rope.'

Dad came running out of the house with a long rope. Vlad took one end and flew with it up to the window. Soon the fire engine came down the street, sirens howling. The whole street woke up and poured out of their houses to watch the fire being put out. They arrived just in time to see young Mandy and Sharon Brown slide down the rope Vlad had taken up to them. Soon the fire was out and word got round that Vlad had spotted the blaze and called the fire brigade and helped rescue the young Browns. Vlad sat on top of the fireman's hat and waved and smiled.

'Good old Vlad,' the crowd called. 'Lucky you were here.'

'It certainly was,' agreed Vlad. 'How any street manages without a resident vampire, I shall never know.'

'We've decided that you can stay on if you want,' said Pete Mercer.

'Thank you, thank you,' smiled Vlad. 'I *would* like to stay on for a bit longer. If it's all right with the Stones, that is.'

'Well, it's not,' said Dad. 'There's too much excitement with you around.'

'I want to stay,' insisted Vlad. 'After all I've done, you can't refuse. Poor Old Vlad, Poor Little Drac.'

Somebody in the crowd shouted, 'Three cheers for Vlad. Hip, hip, hooray.'

Everyone joined in 'Hooray.'

'Did you hear that?' said Vlad, smiling delightedly. '*They* all seem to like me. Now you'll *have* to let me stay.'

'No way,' said Dad firmly. 'You are going home as arranged and that's that.'

'It's not fair,' moaned Vlad. 'What's the point of me being good if you send me away anyway. I'll find a way to stay, whatever you say — you see if I don't.'

10

Vampires

Judy picked up the post from the mat by the front door.

'A bill for you, Dad,' she said. 'And all the rest is for Vlad.'

'Who keeps writing to Vlad?' asked her father.

'It's Mrs Vlad,' replied Judy. 'But Vlad just ignores them.'

'Very odd,' commented her father. 'And talking of Vlad, where is that wretched vampire?'

'Down in the cellar, as usual,' Judy told him.

'I wish I knew what it was in that trunk that keeps him so occupied,' mused her father. 'Have you ever had a peep?'

'I tried,' confessed Judy. 'And so did Paul, but Vlad seemed to appear from nowhere and carry on in the most alarming way, so I gave up.'

'My experience exactly,' said Dad. 'And your mother's. Vlad must be storing something in our cellar that he is determined none of us will know about.'

'What do you think it is?' asked Judy.

'Haven't got a clue,' mused her father. 'But whatever it is, my sixth sense tells me that that's why Vlad is so reluctant to go home.'

'Could be,' said Judy, nodding.

'Yes,' said Dad, grinning, 'and if I were to get rid of the trunk, maybe Vlad would go and leave us in peace.'

'He is behaving very oddly,' remarked Judy.

'Huh,' said her father. 'And when did he behave any other way?'

'But not the usual kind of odd,' Judy explained. 'He's trying to behave like a real vampire. Look at my neck, he tried to bite me in the night.'

Dad looked.

'Bite marks,' he exclaimed. 'Suzanne, come and look at what Vlad has done to Judy,' he called to Mum.

Mum came in carrying Zoë and Dad showed her Judy's neck.

'Look,' he said.

'Mmm,' agreed Mum. 'They do look like vampire bites. I think I've got one too. You look.'

'Yes,' said Dad, 'you have. Let's take a look at Zoë.'

So they looked at the sleeping baby's neck.

'Yes, her too,' said Mum. 'Let's have a look at your neck, Nick. No, you're lucky, he didn't get you.'

'He's got to go,' insisted Dad. 'This is too much. First he drives me crazy, then he antagonizes all the neighbours and now he goes around pretending to bite people. I'm a patient man but this is too much. Quiet everyone. Is that the sound of the refuse truck?' he asked.

'Yes,' said Judy. 'Why?'

'Where's Vlad?' demanded Dad. 'Is he still down in the cellar?'

'No,' said Mum, looking bemused. 'He went upstairs.'

'Good,' said Dad, grinning. 'In that case, I am about to give Vlad's precious trunk to the refuse collectors and then, who knows, maybe he will go home.'

'You can't do that, Dad,' cried Judy. 'It's not fair.'

'You're right,' agreed her father. 'But Vlad is never fair to me and if I'm fair to him I'm at a permanent disadvantage. Out of my way, Judy, I am determined to get rid of that trunk and nothing and no one is going to stop me.'

Judy and Mum heard Dad open the cellar door

and go down. Then they heard the bumping of the trunk, as he dragged it upstairs.

'No good trying to stop him,' said Mum. 'You know what he's like when he's determined.'

'Vlad will be so upset,' said Judy. 'And he was very brave in the fire and *I* want to know what was in that trunk and now I never will.'

'I know, love,' agreed her mother. 'I'm dying to know, too. But Vlad must go home, he's just too disruptive to our lives. And I can't cope with Vlad and Zoë at the same time. You must understand that.'

'I do,' said Judy reluctantly. 'Poor old Vlad, he does try to please people but he gets very confused.'

'Look,' said Mum, moving to the window. 'Dad's managed to drag the trunk out.'

'It does look like a coffin, doesn't it?' commented Judy.

'Umm,' said her mother. 'A bit creepy really.'

They watched, fascinated, as the refuse collector lifted up the trunk and dumped it into the back of the van and tried to see what was inside as the teeth of the mechanism began to bite at the trunk.

Vlad flew into the room.

'What are you two looking at?'

'Well, er,' said Mum, 'you see, Vlad, Dad felt the trunk in the cellar was taking up too much space, so he's just paid the refuse men to take it away.'

'What?' shrieked Vlad in dismay. 'When? Where is it now?'

'It got thrown into the truck a minute ago.'

Dad came into the room panting and rubbing his hands.

'I caught them,' he said. 'They took it.'

'Stop them,' yelled Vlad, wringing his hands. 'You've got to make them stop!'

'Why?' demanded Dad. 'What was in the trunk?'

'Ghitza,' said Vlad, tears rolling down his face. 'My son Ghitza!'

'Come on,' yelled Dad and, grabbing Vlad, he raced out of the house and ran as fast as he could after the refuse cart.

'Stop the machine,' he shouted. 'There's someone in the trunk.'

The machine stopped. Vlad, Dad and the dustmen stood and looked at the back of the van. The driver let a flap drop and there, surrounded by potato peelings, old newspapers, apple cores, tea bags, coffee grouts and every kind of rubbish imaginable,

sat a small bad-tempered vampire.

'Papa Vlad,' said the vampire, with a strong Romanian accent. 'I do not like zis place.'

'I don't blame you, son,' said Vlad sympathetically. 'Now come on, out you fly.'

So Ghitza flew out smelling of rubbish and stood next to Dad. He was small, but not as small as Vlad, and much uglier.

'Terribly sorry,' said Dad to the refuse collectors. 'A bit of a misunderstanding — I'd no idea what was in the trunk.'

'You should be ashamed,' the refuse collector shouted at Dad. 'Trying to mash up a little baby vampire like that.'

'I didn't know there was a vampire in the trunk,' said Dad weakly.

'Didn't know?' said the refuse collector aggressively, clenching his fist. 'Didn't know? Pull the other one, it's got bells on. I've a good mind to punch your face in.'

Vlad flew on to Dad's shoulder.

'He really didn't know,' Vlad explained. 'No one knew. I didn't tell a soul. It was my secret.'

'You're Vlad the Drac, aren't you?' asked the refuse collector.

'I most certainly am – the one and only.' And turning to Ghitza he said, 'Did you see that, son, everyone knows me here. Would you like my autograph?'

'Well, yes, I would,' said the refuse man. 'Thank you very much.'

'There,' said Vlad. 'It's your lucky day. I just so happen to have a photograph of myself in my pocket. To my favourite refuse collector from Vlad the Drac.'

'Thank you, thank you very much. Well, I suppose I'd best be getting along. Bye,' said the refuse collector and he drove off.

'We'd better go back to the house,' said Judy.

'Yes,' agreed Dad. 'And Vlad can tell us just what is going on.'

Soon the whole family were gathered in the front room. Ghitza was wrapped in a big towel, while his clothes were in the washing machine.

Paul complained, 'Why didn't someone call me? I missed all the fun.'

'Fun!' exclaimed Vlad. 'You call grasping my son, literally, from the jaws of death, fun? Honestly, people!'

'Papa Vlad,' said Ghitza in a loud voice, 'I do not like zees people.'

'Never mind, son,' said Vlad. 'We're going home soon.'

'I just fail to understand,' began Dad, 'why you brought Ghitza all this way in the first place.'

'To stop vampires becoming extinct, like those poor dinosaurs. You see, Mrs Vlad, I mean Magda, doesn't want to have any more children.'

'Well, five is quite a lot,' commented Mum.

'I don't see what all this has to do with Ghitza being here now,' complained Dad.

'I wanted Ghitza to vampirise Judy and Mum and the snoglet,' explained Vlad.

'Why?' asked Dad in amazement.

'So that they would become vampires and I could take them home with me to Romania and then there would be three more vampires who I like.'

'And what about me?' exclaimed Dad. 'Wasn't I going to get vampirised?'

'Oh *no*,' said Vlad emphatically, pulling a disgusted face. 'I'm not daft. I didn't want *you* in Romania quarrelling with me till the end of time.'

'And what about me?' demanded Paul.

'I was going to leave you behind with Dad,' Vlad explained. 'I'm not selfish. I didn't want Dad to be lonely.'

'I'm begining to understand,' said Mum. 'Ghitza was going to bite us so that we could become vampires, right?'

'Right,' agreed Vlad.

'So it was Ghitza who's been biting people, not you?'

'Correct,' agreed Vlad.

'So why haven't we been turned into vampires then?' demanded Mum.

'Because he's too young and his heart isn't in it. He's a terrible disappointment to me, that boy. He's got a nasty temper but he's no vampire.' Vlad burst into tears. 'I've got nothing left to live for — people will take over completely from vampires. It's too bad.'

'Never mind, Vlad,' said Judy, stroking his head. 'Maybe your children will get worse as they grow up.'

'I most certainly hope so,' said Vlad, wiping his eyes.

'Papa Vlad,' announced Ghitza, 'I am terribly hungry. I vant something to eat.'

'What do you like?' asked Judy. 'Soap, like Papa Vlad?'

'No,' said Ghitza emphatically, 'I don't like soap, I like meat.'

'Oh, I *see*,' said Dad. 'So all that meat was for him.'

'Well, of course,' snapped Vlad. 'It certainly wasn't for me.

'And the vampire the neighbours kept seeing, that was Ghitza too?'

'Yes,' said Vlad. 'But he's no more a real vampire than I am. How I'm going to tell his mother, I don't know.'

'I heard something on the radio this morning,' announced Paul. 'It said there had been a mysterious outbreak of vampire activity in Transylvania.'

'Yes,' said Mum, 'there was something about it in the paper, too. I meant to keep it for Vlad.'

'Maybe Mrs Vlad has something to say about it in all the letters and emails she's been sending you and that you couldn't be bothered to open,' Judy suggested.

'Get them,' demanded Vlad. 'Quick, quick, hurry, hurry.'

Judy went and fetched them. Vlad read through them. He began to grin broadly.

'She thinks it's one of the other children. She's not sure which, but she suspects it's our son Dad (that's a pity, wish it had been one of the others but never mind). I must go home immediately, not a moment to lose. Once again, there are vampires in Transylvania. Oh, Great Uncle Ghitza, thou shouldst be living at this hour. Come Judith, help me pack. I'll catch the plane this afternoon after all.'

As Vlad packed he sang:

'Blood, blood, glorious blood,
Nothing quite like it for mixing with mud.'

Judy and Paul sat in the front room and looked at Ghitza.

'Papa Vlad,' he told them, 'he no like me any more.'

'Oh, I'm sure he does,' remonstrated Judy. 'It's just that your not being a real vampire has come as a shock to him.'

'What would you like to do while Papa Vlad is packing?' asked Paul, thinking that they should take Ghitza's mind off his father.

'I like very much the toy in your room,' Ghitza told him.

'So it was you playing with my computer,' said Paul.

'Yes, it was I. I like this toy very much. You show me how to use, please.'

'Sure,' said Paul. 'We can play games on it together.'

So Paul and Ghitza went off to Paul's room.

Vlad carried on singing while he packed. Then he called out,

'Get me a cab, I'm ready. Not a minute to waste.'

So Dad phoned for a cab and they all gathered outside the house to wave 'Goodbye' to Vlad.

'Bye,' they shouted.

'Bye,' called Vlad as the cab sped away.

As they walked back into the house Dad said, 'Thank God for that. I have never been so glad to see the back of anyone in my life. And I want to make one thing absolutely clear: no member of this family is ever, ever, ever to allow that vampire back into this house. No matter what he says or what he's done or what has happened, I don't want him back. Is that absolutely clear? Is it? Even to you, Judy? You're the weak link in the chain — do you understand?'

'Yes, Dad,' said Judy, sighing.

'Well, I certainly hope so, because if I ever find him in this house again, I shall do something terrible to the person who invited him.'

As they entered the house they heard a sound.

'Someone left the television on,' said Mum.

'I didn't,' said Paul.

'Nor me,' echoed Judy.

They ran into the front room and there in front

of the TV sat Ghitza watching intently.

'This toy, I like very, much also,' he told the Stones.

'*What* are *you* doing here?' demanded Dad, his head in his hands.

'I don't like to go with Papa Vlad to Romania,' announced Ghitza. 'I like much more to stay here with you. I like to play with computer toy upstairs. This I like very much.'

The Stones stared at him in horror. Then Dad grabbed the phone.

'Is that London Airport? Good. Put me through to the departure lounge. Hello, this is Nicholas Stone here. It's very urgent — you have to stop one of your passengers boarding his plane to Romania. This is a matter of the utmost urgency. Under no circumstances must Vlad the Drac be allowed to leave the country until he has collected a very valuable piece of luggage he left behind. The message is "Stop that vampire." Yes, send him back here immediately. No need to tell him why, just send him.'

'But, Dad,' objected Judy. 'You said that no one in the house . . .'

'Never, mind about that,' snapped Dad. 'This is an emergency.'

They sat and waited anxiously. About an hour

later a cab drew up and Vlad flew out and over to the letter-box.

'Coo-ee,' he called through the letter-box. 'Anyone at home? I'm back. I knew you'd find you couldn't live without me. Mrs Vlad will have to handle the situation in Transylvania. You don't have a thing to worry about 'cos I'm ba-ack.'

About the Author

Ann Jungman was born in London where she still lives. After training as a lawyer, Ann did some primary school teaching and that led directly to writing for children. Ann is the author of more than a hundred books ranging from picture books to full length novels.

Ann is also the director of Barn Owl Books and spends part of each year in Australia.

VLAD THE DRAC RETURNS
by Ann Jungman

£4.99 ISBN 1-903015-34-0

Vlad the Drac, the tiny vegetarian vampire, is back. Now that he is no longer a secret, Vlad wants his photo in the papers every day and to be on T.V. as much as possible. The vampire's antics to get publicity get him into lots of trouble but when he goes missing, everyone is very worried.

"Funny, unpredictable, playful and defiant, Vlad is always excellent company" –
Nicholas Tucker in *The Rough Guide to Children's Books*

VLAD THE DRAC SUPERSTAR
by Ann Jungman

£4.99 ISBN 1-903015-45-6

The diminutive vampire Vlad the Drac is back in London, this time to star in his first film, *Marauding Monsters of the Outer Galaxy*. Paul and Judy persuade their parents to let Vlad come and live with them. It is a decision they soon come to regret, for Vlad not only disrupts the whole film studio but becomes vastly too big for his boots at home as well.

"With this vampire, it's not your neck you have to worry about but your giggle box — laugh, I nearly died!" — *Michael Rosen*